MAYBE NOW

MAYBE NOW

MAYBE THIS TIME

JOLIE MOORE

MOORE DIGITAL
MDM MEDIA INC

This edition published by

Moore Digital Media Inc
1125 N Fairfax Avenue
Unit #46071
West Hollywood, CA 90046

Cover Designer: Cover Me Darling
eISBN: 978-1-64414-081-9
ISBN: 978-1-64414-082-6

A NOTE ABOUT MAYBE NOW

This book features over thirty comics from Zoe Andreis. They can also be viewed in full color at high resolution at zoeandreis.com. Thanks for reading. We hope you enjoy the story.

ONE

Zoe

"I'm up here," Zoe Andreis said to the bus driver. She glanced down at her T-shirt, where the bus driver's eyes appeared to have settled, then back up at him.

Note to self: don't wear words and pictures across your breasts while on the bus in Los Angeles. Not if you don't want men to look.

"Ma'am, for the record, I wasn't looking at your T-shirt. I was looking to make sure you didn't bang your head," the driver said. His deep voice rumbled along with the motor. Both sounds reverberated through her chest.

Zoe tilted her head to suss out what he was talking about and promptly banged her head on the metal grab bar. Were buses in Los Angeles made for short people? She couldn't be the only five foot eleven person to ever get in one of these orange behemoths. Not for the first time she wondered how in the hell tall men got through the world without constant goose eggs and a large tube of Arnica on hand because she wasn't doing so well.

Rubbing her head, she looked at the driver. "Fine, you weren't looking at my...shirt. How much do I owe you?"

"What it says there on the box." His large hand tapped against the fare box. "You owe MTA a dollar seventy-five."

"Geez, that much?" she asked. Seemed like a lot for a slow bus on an even slower timetable.

"Ma'am, I have a schedule," he said, pointing to a computer screen mounted on the windshield. "You can pay the fare or not, but you need to decide in the next five seconds."

Zoe dug the change she been saving for laundry from her wallet and dropped seven quarters in the box, all the while shaking her head. Following the lead of the other passengers, she jammed ear buds in her ears and took the only seat available, across from the ornery bus driver.

If she were *driving* neither the T-shirt, nor the necessary quarters would have been an issue. But those pesky laws about having a current driver's license in any of the United States were getting in the way of that. Well, that and not having a car. And the fact that she wasn't sure she was going to be in Los Angeles for more than a couple of months. And the fact that if she were only going to be here for a little while, she'd rather spend that time with her family and not standing in some interminable DMV line.

She pulled her phone from her purse and tapped furiously to bring up the route information before she missed her stop. "I have to get off at Clark Street. Can you let me know where that is?"

A tanned hand bent a microphone, his blunt-tipped finger beat against the mesh top. The sound reverberated through the bus, penetrating through the silicone in her ears.

"Gotcha covered, Wanderlust."

How did he…? She looked down at her T-shirt for the second time that morning.

Riiiight.

The shirt. The cartoon tee was the only clean thing from her hastily packed duffle. She hated the shirt and the compromise of principles it represented. But until she bought some kind of laundry detergent and collected even more quarters, it had the single most important quality in a shirt—it was clean. While the bus lumbered through the heavy rush hour traffic, Zoe spied a patch on a navy blue jacket hung on the back of the driver's seat. It matched the patch on his uniform blue short-sleeved shirt: 27912.

"Thanks, two seven nine one two," she said and jammed the ear buds in tighter.

When the podcast went quiet twenty minutes later, she glanced at the driver again. As she got closer to the stop her app promised was close to the hospital, she wondered if 27912 had a name. He was the first driver she'd seen this week who hadn't been on the verge of retirement. Cocking her head to peer at him while not looking like she was spying, Zoe guessed his age at something south of fifty. Grunts of protest filled the air when the bus jolted to a stop. She looked through the mammoth windshield to see a sporty little luxury car zip across three lanes before making a left and disappearing. Zoe looked from the wisp of the car's exhaust to the bus driver. His hazel eyes didn't blink. He turned the enormous wheel, pushed at the gas and steered back into the choked traffic.

Doing quick math in her head, Zoe figured she'd ridden on hundreds of busses over the last ten years. The blue and yellow buses in Athens with the destinations all in Greek. She laughed as she remembered that her 'It's all Greek to me' panel was still one of the most popular.

WANDERLUST

By Zöe Andreis

The bright purple and turquoise buses in Istanbul. And the myriad of blue buses in Budapest. In all that time, she'd never noticed a bus driver before. Had never seen anyone nearly as young as she. But they couldn't turn into old guys overnight, she reasoned. Maybe she'd been too worried about getting lost in whatever foreign city she called home to notice their age.

Young ones must exist in the wild and she'd spotted

one. Most bus drivers of her admittedly hazy memory were a blur of predominantly men, and the occasional woman, whose job it was to get her where she was going. Zoe shook her head, clearing it of thoughts about destination. The last thing she wanted to think about was where she was going.

The driver glanced right at the side mirror. He had those light yellow-green eyes she'd seen often in Eastern Europeans and middle easterners. Out of habit, Zoe smiled at 27912. She made a point of being nice to people doing hard jobs. Harder than hers anyway. Which was about ninety-nine percent of the population. She sat down all day at her big desk surrounded by pencils, fountain pens, and thin paint brushes and tried to find the humor in her everyday life. It sometimes made her brain hurt. But it was by no means digging ditches or driving a bus.

The closer she got to Cedars, the more the worry set in. Papa hadn't been himself since the moment she'd landed from her sixteen-hour flight and schlepped her large nylon backpack, not to her brother's new house, but straight to the hospital. She'd been grateful that Papa hadn't been on the deathbed her brother had intimated over Skype.

The presence of his pale face and the absence of his usual acerbic wit had been disconcerting. It was then, for the first time, she thought about the possibility that her father, a fixture in her life, might not live forever. Losing her mother to cancer had been hard enough. Adult orphan wasn't a moniker she wanted to carry.

"Clark Street," 27912 mouthed into the microphone. The bus cruised along at a regular speed.

That was her cue. She stood, protecting her head with her right hand this time, and waited for the bus brakes to grind to a halt. Even with lip biting and rapid blinking, tears welled in her eyes. Damn. She wasn't going to do this. She had to get it together before she got to her dad's room. It was time for her to be the strong one in the family.

"You okay, Wanderlust?" the driver asked.

"Zoe from Chicago. And yeah, I'm okay. Tired, I guess."

27912 pulled to the shelter marking the end of her ride. "I've got your number, two seven nine one two, what's your name?"

He hesitated a long second. "Max Kiss," he said, pronouncing the name like it would have sounded in its native Hungarian and nothing like the 'kiss' that would be written on paper, but like 'kish' "Drive this route every day. Glad to be of service. Thanks for riding MTA."

"Okay, thanks," Zoe said and took the three steps to the concrete. Max Kiss gave her a two-finger salute before steering back into the metal ribbon of traffic on Sunset Boulevard.

Ha. Ironic.

She'd flown six thousand miles only to run into someone with the same surname as the one listed under hers on the bell for her apartment in Budapest's Seventh District.

Small world.

Tugging her daypack higher, Zoe made her way from Sunset to San Vicente for part two of her trip. Cedars-Sinai scrolled on the marquis of the bus that arrived at the royal blue shelter. There wasn't any mystery about its destination this time. Watching her head, she stepped onto the little West Hollywood City Ride bus. The cool interior was full of men and women in scrubs on their way to work and older people in need of medical attention.

She stood for the ten-minute ride rather than fold herself into one of the plastic molded seats. Palm trees, coffee shops, and upscale boutiques flew by. On the one hand, being back in the States was a relief. She could read signs and communicate in her native language without constantly second guessing herself. There was no wondering exactly what in the heck a shop sold behind opaque windows, nor was there worry about miscommunication. But gone was the sense of excitement and adventure she usually felt when zipping through whichever foreign city was home at the moment.

By Zöe Andreis

After the walk from the bus stop to the tall modern hospital building, Zoe walked through the automatic doors that opened with a hiss, and then breathed in the cold antiseptic air. Her watch read ten o'clock. Right on time for visiting hours. Hesitating for a long moment, she was jostled toward the elevator bay by those more eager than her to get upstairs. Probably visiting maternity, she reasoned. She'd missed the birth of her niece, not that she would have been bouncing with excitement to see the newborn namesake of her mom. Given the choice now, she thought, she'd happily choose newborn hysteria over the geriatric floor any day. Baby Iris was safe at home with her mother though.

Reluctantly, she pressed the call button. The cargo-sized elevator opened. Letting an orderly with a rolling bed and IV drip go ahead of her, she stepped in and pressed her destination floor. As efficient and as quiet as one of those electric cars everyone seemed to have, she was up on the floor in nearly an instant. This time, the room number was 1418.

Deep breath in.

Whoosh of breath out.

Zoe pushed through the door to her dad's room.

"Ah, jeez. You again," Dominic said before she could close the wide door. "You'da thought I would have died with that look on your face. When are you going back to Budapest or wherever you're laying your head these days?"

"I was thinking of Krakow next, Papa. But I'm staying put in L.A. for now."

"How do you like Nicki's house? He did a pretty good job, huh?"

"Papa—"she started, but her brother's entrance cut her off.

"Speak of the devil. What's it like livin' with your sister again? Been probably a dozen years since the two of you fought over a bathroom. Nicki always did take longer with his hair than you did." Dominic's laugh was half gasp, half wheeze.

"Papa," she raised her voice, "I'm renting a little bungalow in Los Feliz."

"What?" His voice, though a bit hoarse from coughing,

went up a couple of octaves. "How much you shelling out for that? L.A.'s gotten ridiculous over the years."

"I can afford it," Zoe said.

"Why can't you stay with Nicki?"

"Guests. Three-day-old fish. You know," she said, trying to steer clear of the real reason she'd gotten a rental.

"Family ain't fish," Dominic said, pushing past social niceties.

"I ran through my backlog of panels. I needed space to work. Inking is a messy business," Zoe said, giving one excuse after another and holding up her stained hands as exhibit one.

"What about the loft?" her dad persisted.

"Nicki has his editing stuff up there," she retorted.

"Holly needs help with little Iris too, you know. When I was coming up, the whole neighborhood—"

"Papa! Stop. It's okay. Nicki and Holly needed their privacy. I decided after a couple of weeks that living with near newlyweds was a bit much."

Her brother turned red from his neck to the roots of his too-damn-long hair. Served him right. When she accepted the invitation to stay at her brother and sister-in-law's place, she expected the loudest noises to come from her niece, baby Iris. She didn't begrudge her brother sexy times with his cute wife, but by the fifth night she was done. Hovering between being completely grossed out on one hand and jealous on the other, she'd decided that space to work and sleep was paramount.

"Well anyway," her dad said, swiftly changing the subject, "you don't need to stay. I'm doing fine."

"You're *not* fine, Papa. You've been in and out of this place for weeks."

"I wish I'd never come in this damned place. It's a racket. Ten thousand dollar scans. Hundred dollar meals. Even the pills cost more than a cup of coffee. Construction was the wrong business. I shoulda convinced Alex to change horses—"

"You're here, Dad, because Gemma Hart found you on the floor of her Malibu house panting like a dog," Nicki said like it wasn't the first time.

"Gemma Hart? The recluse actress?" Zoe said, trying to recall what she'd read about the British transplant in an airplane magazine.

Nicki's nod wasn't charitable. "Yeah, her."

"I thought she lived in a bunker or something. No one's seen her since she won that Academy Award a million years ago."

"Her bunker is a fixer upper in Malibu. But I shouldn't have said anything. Dad had to sign an NDA."

"Yeah, well. I wasn't too damn good at keeping that secret," Dominic said on a cough.

"You said you were working on some small project, Papa. Emphasis on small."

"Have you seen Malibu? Some of those houses sit cheek and jowl. It's not some mansion. It was small enough that I could do the major carpentry and sub out the rest. Adonis has it covered now."

It wasn't until she felt the scratch of her own fingernails against her neck that Zoe realized she was having a hard time swallowing. The pressure was starting to get to her.

"I'm sure it'll be great," she said while using her right hand to ease the growing knot in her neck. "Is he working over there now?" Zoe couldn't keep the disdain from her voice.

"You haven't seen him?" Dominic asked, as if she and her oldest brother were the best of friends. She hadn't seen him for going on five years. Hadn't shared more than a perfunctory greeting in more than a decade.

"I don't have a car," she said, trying to inject a note of warning into her voice. The subject of Adonis Andreis was strictly off limits.

"Funny how you get here every damned day."

"Papa, let's not talk about this."

"What? That you haven't said more than 'hidey ho' to your brother in twelve years?"

"It's fine. Papa. We're fine. Maybe I'll call him and we can have coffee."

"He doesn't drink coffee."

"A beer then," Zoe said before she could stop herself.

"Zoe—"

She was saved from yelling by the swishing door. A man and a woman swooped in on an air current.

They introduced themselves as staff cardiologists. Dr. Gretchen Pearson appeared to be in charge and did all the talking for the white coated duo. For ten minutes, they asked rapid-fire questions about Papa's diet, his family history, and the symptoms that kept him coming back to the hospital.

"So we're going to send you home today, Mr. Andreis," Dr. Pearson concluded.

"That's it?" Zoe asked, her tone nothing short of confrontational.

"No, that's not it," Dr. Pearson answered. "We'll have your dad come to the clinic tomorrow for a stress test."

"The one where he runs on a treadmill?"

"Yes, that. Ms…?"

"Andreis. Like my dad. But what about the tests you've already done?" She was starting to agree with her dad about the cash scan.

WANDERLUST

By Zöe Andreis

Her dad was right, there had to be one hell of a profit in the medical business.

"Those were inconclusive, Ms. Andreis. And I didn't administer those earlier tests. I'm starting again from the ground up. I'll be at the clinic tomorrow to supervise the testing and we'll take it from there."

"But can Dad go back to work now?" Nicki asked. Zoe spared a glance at him. The Malibu actress didn't need her father as much as Zoe did. Contractors were interchangeable. Fathers were not.

"Let's see after tomorrow. I'd recommend you take it easy tonight, Mr. Andreis. We don't want a repeat of any of the earlier incidents."

The 'earlier incidents' were what had brought her here. A landline had come free with the one bedroom apartment she'd rented in Budapest. In the eighteen months she'd been there, the thing had never rung. Zoe had been tucking herself into the duvet fresh from storage in the bottom of her wardrobe. A few glasses of wine and swapping stories with her friend Amelia and the other expats had fueled her creativity. She couldn't wait to get to work on a series on European travel. The train network that was eerily efficient and chaotic at the same time. The discount airlines that didn't allow under-seat storage without cost.

The possibilities had whirred in her brain in the cab from the wine bar to her apartment. A good night's sleep, morning coffee and pastry, and a fruitful workday had beckoned. But not five minutes after she'd snapped off her bedside lamp had she heard bleating. Pulling herself from a doze, Zoe had dug her phone from her bedside drawer. But it was turned off as it had been every other night. Having friends all over the world meant someone would undoubtedly drunk dial her when she was in a deep sleep.

The slippery glass phone dropped from her hands, but the bleating continued. Damn. She stumbled from bed and walked through the chill living room until she saw a red light winking. Her brain stalled a long moment before she realized that it was the free landline that had come with the Internet and cable TV. For the life of her, she couldn't remember sharing the number with anyone. Hell, she didn't even know the number without checking her own contact information on her mobile phone.

"Hello," she blurted into the phone. There was a hesitation on the other end. Damn. Zoe plumbed her mind for the Hungarian words the caller probably wanted. "*Jó estét? Szia?*" she broached.

Something clattered on the other end of the line. Zoe pushed her face closer. "Hello?"

"Sorry. Zoe?"

"Nicki?"

"It's Dad."

With those two little words, she was undone. Papa. Her worst nightmare had come to life. Gripping the phone for dear life, she braced herself for the inevitable news that she'd become an orphan—at thirty-two. "Tell me."

"He's fine, sis."

"Fine?!" she yelled into the little plastic gadget.

"He's not dead. He collapsed on a job site. The homeowner called an ambulance. He's here at the hospital now."

"Put him on," Zoe demanded. She needed to hear from the ornery man for herself.

"I can't right now. He's out for some kind of chest x-ray or something. I just wanted you to know."

"Did he have a heart attack?"

"They haven't ruled it out. His client said he couldn't breathe and then he came here. That's all I know."

"Do I need to come home?"

"That's up to you," Nicki had said. "Adonis is here."

Her other brother's name nearly stopped her own heart. But it wouldn't do to have two cardiac patients in the family. "I'll come. I'll get the first flight to Frankfurt or Amsterdam and figure it out from there."

"Holly or I will come pick you up at the airport," Nicki said with relief. She'd made the right decision.

Zoe had placed the phone back in the cradle. That wine induced good night's sleep never came. She spent the next two hours booking a flight to Zurich. In the brief time before she'd left the apartment, Zoe scanned in completed panels and emailed them to her editor. Her pens and emergency clothes filled her backpack. In the first light of dawn, she navigated the train and bus that would take her to the airport.

Three weeks later, she was standing in a different room in another hospital, no closer to finding an answer than they had been that first night he'd been admitted.

When Dr. Pearson and her acolyte had left, Zoe got closer to the bed. She grabbed her dad's hand.

"Don't die on me, okay Papa?"

"Ah, for Christ's sake. Don't you start crying. I'm not going anywhere. Iris needs a grandfather."

TWO

Max

Max hunched over the desk and carefully installed the cannon pinion over the center post. With the tweezers in his right hand, he pushed down gently. Next, the hour wheel and dial slipped into place. The watch's hands, he meticulously placed in the twelve o'clock position, making sure the horizontal alignment was perfect. Standing from his solid oak rolling chair, Max squatted at eye level. Yes, the Rolex's hands were level. A tiny sliver of space cast a slim shadow between the face and the hands. Satisfied that the minute and hour hands weren't bent or resting against the markers, he replaced the crystal. The click of the case snapping shut was the most satisfying sound he'd heard that morning.

Checking the time on the Mondaine on the wall, he turned the hands on the watch to match. Pushing in the crown, Max waited for an interminable heartbeat. Then he lifted the piece to his ear. The precise ticking off of seconds was as reassuring as a baby's first heartbeat.

Noticing the time, he hurried to pick up the pins and add the black leather strap. With swift movements, he snapped the strap into place and buckled the timepiece to his wrist. His tiny house was small enough that he made it to his bedroom in seconds. After discarding his robe, he slipped into the navy blue shorts and short sleeved button down shirt of his MTA uniform. Grabbing his jacket while on the way out, he made sure the house was alarmed and slipped through the back door into the alley where he kept his car.

The car display lit up. Ringing filled his car. He glanced from the bumper-to-bumper traffic to the caller I.D., Miklós Kiss.

Édes apa.

His father.

"Where are you, Max?" His dad's tone was belligerent. One deep breath. Two. Three. Then he spoke.

"I'm in my car on my way to work."

"I can't get the stove to work. I want toast for breakfast!"

"Dad. Turn off the oven."

"What?"

"Make sure all the knobs line up. The word 'off' should be at the top of all five knobs."

"Hold on."

Max held on. He was out of sick days. Out of personal days. Family leave required planning. There was no way he could rush up to Santa Clarita to check on the gas stove at his father's house. He was going to have to manage this from his car. And hope his father didn't blow himself and the entire neighborhood to kingdom come.

"Dad? *Apa*!"

Clattering of plastic receiver against the wall. His dad was using the hardwired phone his parents had installed nearly forty years ago.

"It's off. I double checked. How do I get toast? You haven't answered that one."

"Use the toaster I bought you two months ago," he said before he could filter the exasperation from his voice.

"Toaster?"

"Look on the left side of the kitchen," he said, swerving around some guy who looked like he was reading a magazine. Angelenos had taken multi-tasking to a whole new level. "Next to the drain board."

"God damn it. Why didn't you tell me about this before?"

Max resisted the urge to yell back. Of course he'd told his father about the toaster. He'd stood with Miklós in the kitchen reviewing the instructions. He'd watched his father make and eat that first batch of toast.

"You know now, Dad. Get the bread from the fridge. There's butter on the counter."

"Where's the *kenyérszalonna*?"

The Hungarian bacon without a hint of bacon in it was hard to get in California's health-obsessed markets. "That's not an American food, *Apa*. I'll look a little harder. But for now there's butter, okay?"

"Fine. I'm hungry enough to eat this," Miklós said before the phone clattered in the bracket.

Looking at the watch helped calm Max. He wouldn't let his dad or the morning's traffic snarl make a dent in his mood today because the 1960 Rolex Oyster Date was keeping time like a champ.

With no further calls from his father, he knew he'd dodged a bullet today. He could kick the can of part-time or round-the-clock care down the road a little bit further.

Maybe the watch had brought him a little bit of good luck. He'd made it in early for his shift, no problem.

"You want to switch routes?" Carl Fonseca asked when he got to MTA's depot in Sun Valley.

Carl had one of the most coveted routes, not because it was the prettiest or safest, but because the layover at the corner of Van Nuys and Moorpark was right next to an In-n-Out Burger. It was what Carl had gotten with a ton of seniority and serious maneuvering.

"I'm good," Max said, trying not to think about the fresh made-to-order burger he'd be missing. Instead he was focused on the extreme unlikelihood he'd see Zoe again. The sliver of a chance had him banking on the forgettable lunch options of his regular route. He'd trade the burger for the chance of a little bit of sunshine Zoe could bring to his day. He'd been caring for his parents for so long that he'd forgotten what it was like to have a little bit of a crush on someone. To be a bit eager for a glimpse of an attractive woman. "I like the chicken wraps from the place on Sunset fine," he said in response to Carl's perplexed look.

"Just wanted to say thanks for covering for me when my wife was sick."

"Make me the offer again in a couple of weeks," Max said, sure he'd be more appreciative when Zoe faded from his memory. Or when he needed to switch for an appointment with the gerontologist he'd found for his dad.

He had a quick look at the local construction notices and traffic alerts then found his assigned bus in the lot. As he adjusted the seat and made sure the computer and microphone were working, he thought about the stop on the corner of Sunset Boulevard and Fountain Avenue. He wondered if the long-legged woman with the cartoon shirt would be there today. Maybe she'd only gone to the hospital that one day.

Tall, assertive women weren't his usual cup of tea. But his heart had done a funny little flip when she'd tried to keep back tears. He remembered that feeling when his mom's hospital stay stopped being temporary. When a cadre of doctors, nurses, and social workers had descended on him with words like nursing homes, care centers, and finally — hospice.

As he watched a red light turn to green, he figured he was probably projecting. She was most likely visiting a friend with a baby or something. The baby would go home, and Zoe would never ride the bus again. There were a lot of one-timers. The regulars, the immigrant workforce took the bus every day. They had no vacation. They had no holidays. Those riders were there when it rained, when the weather dipped below fifty, and when the Santa Ana winds blew in a desert-dry heat.

Women like her, though, who didn't know the fare or where the buses were going, were one in a thousand. She had probably been swayed by all the MTA public relations mumbo jumbo that would have been better served padding operator salaries. People like that, they tried a train or a bus once. He'd hear them laughing in the back about the novelty of public transportation in Los Angeles, then they'd get off at the Pantages for a musical, or at the Coliseum for a USC football game, then you'd never see them again. They'd drive next time like they'd done every time before.

Max had psyched himself out so fully, that he nearly ran the larger rubber tires up onto the curb when he saw Zoe standing under the bus shelter plastered with the latest movie posters.

He swallowed then pressed the button opening the front door.

"Good morning." He tried for conversational. Might not have got the tone right.

"Thanks. Not so good for me. Back to Cedars. One seventy-five right?"

"Yep. Fare's the same," he said. Lame. So damned lame. He'd win the contest for lame. Pushing the button to close the door, he looked up to a solid red light.

The woman chose the same seat as she had the day before—across from him. At successive red lights, Max noticed all the things he'd missed yesterday. That she had silver rings on her thumbs, and turquoise beads on her wrists. Her short hair was brushed to the side, exposing her whole face. She looked like a Greek goddess with her strong nose and full lips. He shifted in his seat. Zoe Wanderlust who wasn't his type was certainly moving things around down there like she was.

"Zoe, right?" he asked when the light turned green and he could focus on the traffic in front of him, and not the sharp cheekbones under her golden skin.

22

"And you're Max. Is your family Hungarian?" she asked.

"Yep. They came here after the fifty-six revolution. What gave me away?" he asked. Not a single person ever landed on Hungarian in the popular guess your background game.

"Kiss," she said pronouncing his name right. Everyone else thought his name was literally 'Kiss.' Damn he didn't want to think about kissing now. He'd miss the next stop if his thoughts turned that way. "You pronounced it like everyone does in Budapest," she said.

"Have you been to Budapest?" he asked. He'd been once or twice when his parents could get a visa. The visit had been half appreciation of European architecture and family reunion and half worry about the native family members being targeted by the state security agency because of visiting foreigners. He hadn't been after the fall of the Iron Curtain.

"I live there," she said.

"Really?" Max pulled to the next stop and let a few passengers on. He watched to make sure they paid, nodded to a few regulars, then started down Sunset again. Usually he watched the traffic as well as wondered about the business of Hollywood played out in the unglamorous looking buildings set behind the tall palms. But today, he couldn't care less about television studios, outsized billboards, or 'the industry' he knew nothing about.

"Sure. I'm in the Seventh District." She rolled her eyes after that comment.

"The old Jewish quarter," he said trying to figure out

why she'd rolled her eyes. Bigotry wasn't on the list of traits he liked in a woman.

"I don't know if you've been there in the last two years, but if not, you probably wouldn't recognize it. It's all ruin pubs, and *sörözők, borozók, és drága cukrászdák*."

Pubs, wine bars, and expensive pastry shops, he translated in his head. "You speak Hungarian?" he asked. Some said it was the most difficult language in the world. He didn't know if that was true, since his parents spoke it fluently and he somewhat less so.

Zoe threw her head back and laughed, loud and full throated. Nothing dainty or unassuming about her. The silver bracelets on her wrists jingled as she swept her short bangs from where they'd fallen.

"*Egy kicsit.*" A little. "God, no. Enough to order coffee, pastry, and dinner. I'm never in a city long enough to learn a whole new language. Except Greek. That I learned for my dad," she finished, her earlier laughter gone.

"Who's at Cedars?" he asked though he could already guess the answer from the sober lines of her face.

"My dad's having a stress test today."

"Heart trouble?" he asked. He'd been down that road one too many times.

"Don't know. Been weeks of inconclusive tests."

Max pulled to another stop. Let on a long line of people. Had to turn a few back whose TAP cards and pockets were empty. He looked over to make sure Zoe was still there. That she hadn't been an apparition. Glancing at his newly repaired watch, he calculated ten more minutes until she got off. Before she disappeared back into the mass of Angelenos. It was highly probable that after today he'd never see her again. In a city where everyone was in a vehicle of some sort for hours a day, casual encounters with people you knew didn't happen too often.

He swerved around what looked like an inebriated pedestrian and contemplated his choices. He could do what he'd never done in all the years he'd had the job—ask for her number. He could hope that she gave him a card or something. Card? What was he thinking? She wasn't a lawyer that he could see. He didn't imagine most lawyers were wearing cartoon T-shirts or riding buses. She was a woman temporarily visiting from Europe going to see her dad in the hospital.

For two traffic-chocked blocks he warred with himself. Would asking a woman out while her father was sick be the lowest of the low?

"So are there any Hungarian restaurants in L.A.? I kind of have a craving for *hús leves*," she asked, giving him the opening he needed.

"There's a new place in Hollywood I've been meaning to check out." He kept his tone cautious, walking the line between asking her out and giving her only the facts, Joe Friday style.

Max lifted his foot from the gas, risking delay on the route to give him a few moments more with her.

Zoe opened her backpack and tore a piece of paper from a notebook. Hastily she scribbled and tore the white scrap from the little pad. She extended her hand toward him. He took a hand off the wheel and accepted the slip.

Then a scream erupted from the back of the bus. Looking for a safe opening in the line of cars trying to move to the left lane at the last minute, he pulled the bus to the Clark Avenue stop.

After unbuckling himself from his seat, he sprinted down the aisle toward the gathering passengers.

"Step aside, please," Max said with all the authority he could muster. The tight circle of onlookers parted like the Red Sea. His eyes immediately zeroed in on one of his regulars. The older man was sweating profusely. His right hand had a tight grasp on his left arm as if trying to ease pain. Classic signs of a heart attack. If Max had been drilled in the symptoms once, he'd been drilled a thousand times in the last years.

"You," he pointed at a woman in a wrinkled blue jacket with a cell phone in her hand. "Call nine-one-one. Tell them we have a possible heart attack. We're on the corner of Sunset Boulevard, Clark and San Vicente. Bus number two nine six. Got that?"

The woman nodded hesitantly, but made no move to dial the phone.

"Call now!" Zoe exclaimed. To Max she asked, "What can I do to help?"

"Sit with him. Does anyone know his name?" A lot of head shaking. These people all rode the same buses for years and never exchanged one bit of personal information. Damned modern world of cell phones and ear buds. "I have to call dispatch. Let them know we have a problem. Get a replacement bus out here."

While he placed the call to dispatch, he opened the back doors so those who needed to be somewhere could get off the bus. He was usually very meticulous about keeping a schedule because work and school were important to his passengers. But life and death was more so.

"Max!" Zoe called out. "He's unconscious."

Damn. He dropped the phone and ran back. "Help me get him down on the floor."

Zoe slipped off her backpack and used it as a pillow for the man's head. Another passenger unzipped the man's jacket. A wallet fell to the ground.

"Luis Varga," Zoe read from the man's identification.

"Mr. Varga, an ambulance is coming. You'll be in the hospital soon," he said, though it was very possible the man couldn't hear a thing. Taking in what he'd been drilled to observe, Max watched the rising and falling of the man's chest come to a complete stop. Damn. This guy couldn't die on his bus. No one deserved to end his life that way.

He leaned toward the man's ear.

"Are you okay?"

No response.

Like he'd been taught, he placed one hand flat on the man's chest, interlaced that hand with the fingers of the other, tilted his body over the passenger's, then pressed down. Up and down went his hands for what seemed like forever. The normal response time of the Los Angeles emergency responders was over six minutes. That had been discussed months ago in some safety briefing he'd half tuned out. But Max had never thought about how interminable that would feel in a real life emergency.

"Do you need me to take over?" Zoe offered.

"No. I need to do this. Do you—"

The familiar sound of wailing sirens cut him off.

"The fire department is here," the wrinkle-jacketed passenger announced.

Max kept to his task, making sure there was no pause in his compressions. Consistency was the key with CPR. Five seconds later, a pair of latex gloved hands replaced his. Two other men brought a folding stretcher in the back door. In seconds, the unconscious man was loaded onto the rolling bed and whisked away.

"At least Cedars is close by," Zoe said, looking him in the eye.

He was about to thank her for keeping calm, when a squad of blue, black, and red SUVs arrived. Police, more firefighters, and MTA brass flooded the scene. Max stepped off the bus to talk to the suits gathered at the corner.

It was a full hour before everyone was satisfied with Max's story. The police dismissed foul play. The fire-fighters took their oversized trucks back to the station. The MTA officers felt comfortable that liability wasn't going to rest on their shoulders. The upshot, the MTA brass told him that he could go home for that day. As long as he filled in a thousand forms, some for MTA, some for insurance, detailing exactly what had happened before he left.

Hungry, thirsty, and beat, he finally boarded the bus. He kicked at something that crinkled. Operators weren't responsible for cleaning at the end of a shift, but he didn't like to ride with empty bottles and other trash rolling around. He leaned to pick up the offending scrap and crumpled it into a ball, ready to throw it into the little trash bag he kept on the side of his seat. Something stuck in his brain after he sat. Instead of tossing it, he smoothed the paper flat on his thigh.

Zoe's name and number were written in strong bold strokes. He folded it, more carefully this time, and inserted the paper into a secure pocket in his wallet. If there was anything to be learned from his mother, his father, or today's incident, it was that there was no time to waste. He'd call her this afternoon, the minute he'd dotted the last 'i', crossed the last 't' and signed his name.

THREE

Zoe

When Zoe should have turned left toward Cardiac Care, she turned right toward the Emergency Department.

"Excuse me," she said to a woman behind a large glass window. "Was a Luis Varga admitted?"

The woman's eyes shifted. She bit her lip, but didn't answer. Zoe pressed on.

"I was on the bus when he collapsed. I wanted to see how he was doing. Make sure his family could come," she said, peering around the crowded waiting room for people who looked like Mr. Varga. "I'd be more than happy to speak with them if they have any questions."

"He's not admitted," the woman said finally.

"But the ambulance driver said he was taking Varga to Cedars. We were only a few blocks away when he collapsed." For a moment Zoe considered that she'd gotten it all wrong. Los Angeles was sometimes as foreign to her as Budapest was to most Americans. "I'm in the right place, aren't I?"

The intake nurse sucked in air, lifting her chest and name tag in unison. The sigh following was long and deep.

"I'm sorry to inform you that Mr. Varga didn't make it. He was pronounced dead on arrival."

"Oh," Zoe said, bringing her hand to her mouth. "Oh. God. I'm sorry. So, so sorry."

She backed out of the cramped lobby as fast as her legs would carry her.

Papa.

Dominic had to be okay. She wasn't ready to live without him. Suddenly, seeing her dad was the most important thing she could do in that moment to separate herself from fear of death. Sprinting across the open hospital campus and back through to the building she should have been in from the beginning, Zoe followed the set of signs and multi-colored paint stripes to the small waiting area for the cardiac clinic. This desk clerk, more jovial than the last, directed her to room five. With a smile like that, Zoe knew her dad had to be alive.

"I'm sorry I'm late, Papa," Zoe said as she rushed to her father's side. He was prone on a small gurney. His eyes were closed. She shook him gently, the fear of sudden, rapid, irreversible death omnipresent. "Did they do the test yet?"

The sight of her father in a hospital bed was becoming all too commonplace. He was as still as a corpse, white electrodes pasted to his half-shaved chest. She shook him again. Finally, he raised a single lid. His eye focused on her like a green laser.

"Shhh with all those questions. I'm supposed to be resting."

"Did it hurt? Did you collapse?"

"I'm not quite that old or dead, my dear Zoe," he said with a pained half-smile.

"Don't joke about that, Papa," she admonished, the sight of Luis Varga's collapse still fresh in her mind.

"You know that I'm not going to live forever, right Zoe girl?" her father's normally jokey voice was as serious as cancer.

"None of us are going to live forever," she admitted reluctantly. "But I plan for you to live a bit longer."

"When I'm gone, you're only going to have your brothers."

"If this is about staying with Nicki, don't start. I needed space to draw and ink without worrying about making a huge mess. You and Mom got on me a million times for staining my bed, the carpet, the curtains. You name it."

"This isn't about that, dear heart. You know what this is about. If I have one dying wish it's that you make up with your *other* brother, Adonis."

The knot in her stomach that had eased when his eye opened, balled up tight once again. Before she could recite the long litany of excuses he'd heard before about her reasons for cutting off her brother, the clatter of clogs joined the swoosh of air that tickled her nape.

"No need to make dying declarations, Mr. Andreis," Dr. Pearson said. "Your stress test appeared normal. You've got a great heart for a man your age."

For a man his age. What did that mean? Didn't he want the heart of a twenty-year-old?

"But that doesn't answer the question, does it?" Zoe said, trying her best to be non-confrontational but failing miserably. "He came in here because he had shortness of breath. He's had every damned test under the sun and you're no closer to diagnosing the problem. Are you?"

"Ms. Andreis, we're not. But medicine isn't as easy as pushing a button on a phone and asking the computerized voice for the solution. We diagnose by elimination. At this point, we've eliminated heart issues."

"I'm feeling better, dear girl," Dominic interjected.

"But that's the pattern, isn't it Papa?" Both his eyes were open now. She stared into a face that was a nearly mirror image of her own. "You feel better until you don't."

"I think Mr. Andreis can go home for the night. Let's let him rest. Unless something happens, we'll make an appointment next week with the geriatric care team we've assembled and go from there," Dr. Pearson said. The doctor and her clogs took their exit.

"Dismissed. I guess." Zoe said. "Where are your clothes, I'll help you."

Dominic pointed to the back of the now closed door. Zoe wasn't unaware of the role reversal many children of aging parents faced as she unzipped a thin disposable black garment bag, then helped her father into a T-shirt and jeans covering his pinstriped boxers.

"I don't think you should be home alone, Papa," she said. Thoughts of him rattling around the bottom half of his duplex worried her. As always, he was in the midst of a project that made the place only marginally habitable. The cobbler's kids may not have had shoes, but she bet they had flushing toilets and working doors. There were many days she'd have traded her shoes for running water.

"I've been living alone for years. I'll be just fine," her dad said.

"I don't like the idea of you by yourself." Images of tripping, falling, and broken hips flooded her mind. "We'll get you home, then I'll get my stuff and stay with you for the weekend," she said. Spilled India ink may go unnoticed with drop cloths everywhere in the guest bedrooms.

"You got a license?" her dad threw back.

"We're not going to get into this now."

"If something happens, who's gonna drive me?"

"That's what nine-one-one is for."

"Call Nicki. I'll stay with them. I could help with little Iris. They could use a night out."

"Fine." Zoe dialed her brother, only to discover he was parking in the hospital's lot. Ten minutes later, her dad and her brother were going home together. Dismissed for the next twenty-four hours at least, Zoe took herself to the main registration desk and ordered a cab. She'd talk some sense into her father in the morning. She was well behind in her work and needed to get some ideas on the page anyway. Her normal six-week buffer had dwindled to two. Unemployed artist wasn't something she aspired to.

Ready to press the taxi dispatch's seven digit number she'd picked from the information sheet, the phone rang in her hand. An unknown 323 number popped onto the screen. Running through the few people she knew in Los Angeles, she concluded it was another number for Holly or Nick. Maybe one of them was at work.

"Hello?" she answered.

"Max Kiss," the voice said. "Wanted to see how you were holding up."

"Fine," Zoe said, a shot of nerves zipping through her. Her slippery fingers nearly dropped the glass-encased phone.

"How's your dad?" The deep voice made its way from her ear, through her chest, to parts lower.

"He's going home. I was on my way home, myself," she said for lack of anything more interesting to share.

"If you're hungry, we could meet at the restaurant I mentioned." His voice was California casual. Her heartbeat was not.

"Is it far?" Zoe asked before she could think up something better to say. This was genius stuff. Hard to believe she'd been writing for the last five years. Her job was all pithy remarks and one-liners. But she was failing miserably here. For some reason sounding smart and funny with this guy was important. Usually she could care less. She saved the funny for the job. Serious was for real life.

"Not too bad. I can pick you up," he was saying into her distracted ear.

WANDERLUST

By Zöe Andreis

"No, no. I'll meet you there in half an hour. I have a ride," Zoe said hurriedly. She needed time to pull herself together before she saw him. A cab ride over would give her a minute to think of something witty to talk about during dinner. After she told him about Luis Varga. Because death wasn't funny.

Max spoke again. This time he gave her the location of the restaurant on Vine Street. It was the same address she gave to taxi dispatch a moment later.

♥

THE CAB EASED to the curb opposite the restaurant, the driver pointed his finger toward the address across the street where a solidly built Max waited. Zoe almost didn't recognize Max Kiss without his uniform.

Unobserved, she watched him. He was leaning against the stucco of the restaurant wall. His folded arms were the first thing she noticed. The late afternoon sun glinted off the light brown hair dusting his forearms. She wondered if he'd gotten strong wrestling that huge steering wheel into submission eight hours a day.

Half his biceps were covered with a green and blue striped polo that did wonders for his eyes. But she suspected he already knew that. He was effortlessly handsome in the way of many European men she'd encountered over the years. She sometimes wondered if they were born with that flair. When Max finally looked up, his eyes found hers and didn't look away. Her heart sped up a little. No, a lot. Hesitation gone, she crossed Vine on the red light and joined him outside the restaurant.

Before she could say hello, he pulled her close for the customary greeting she'd seen on the streets of Europe more times than she could count. Zoe fought with the dizziness his aftershave induced. Maybe it was hunger.

"Good news and bad news," he said after he'd kissed her on both cheeks.

"What's that?"

Max jerked a thumb at the front door of the bustling restaurant. "Rehearsal dinner."

Zoe's chest caved with unexpected sadness. For the twenty minutes in that cramped cab, she'd really been looking forward to dinner with Max. She needed something to get her out of her own head. Conversation about buses or Hungarian food had been a promised lifeline.

"That the bad news, right?"

"Yep," he said, nodding. A small smile played around his lips, crinkling the skin around his yellow eyes, dimpling his cheek.

"What's the good?"

He lifted a white plastic bag from a ledge. The restaurant's logo was emblazoned on the side. There were at least four or five Styrofoam containers stuffed into the bag. "I got take out."

"How'd you do that?"

"I pleaded with the owner in my best Hungarian. Told him it was our first date. He put together a little bit of everything for us."

Zoe could feel heat rushing from her chest to her face. Then she wanted to pinch herself. Who was embarrassed by a date? He was attractive. She wanted to get to know him. This was what adults did before jumping into bed. And she very much wanted to —

"So…where shall we go to enjoy this feast?" she asked, cutting off her train of thought.

"I'm a couple of miles away."

Zoe hesitated for only a second. What in the hell? Life was short. Hungarian food was good. Kissing Max may be even better. "Where's your car? You have a car, right?"

"I don't take the big orange bus everywhere," Max said with a laugh. They walked several feet to a dark red Toyota that was a marriage between a station wagon and an SUV. Max pressed a fob and the car beeped while the door locks sprang open.

"Your chariot awaits," he said with a flourish of his hand.

Zoe had to laugh because it was silly and chivalrous all at the same time. She swung her backpack to the front and buckled herself in. Digging first into one pocket and then another, she released a frustrated sigh.

"What are you looking for?"

"My phone."

"Checking up on your dad?"

"Not now. I'm leaving it all up to my brother tonight. I'm going to text him your name, address, and phone number. You seem lovely, but this isn't Europe. I need backup in case I turn up dead." European newspapers were filled with stories of American serial killers. She didn't know if it was all salacious hype, but it was good to be prepared even if he seemed like a trustworthy guy.

"Fifty-one thirty Raleigh," Max said, easing the car into an alley. The buildings on either side were covered in ivy.

Zoe typed the relevant info into her phone.

"We're here already? That has to be the shortest drive I've ever taken in L.A."

After they both alighted and he rescued their food from the back seat, he locked the car with a beep. "It's through this courtyard," he said.

The ivy-covered wall had a single wood door not covered by any vegetation. It reminded her of a Hobbit house. But Max Kiss was anything but a Hobbit. Unless they made tall, sexy Hobbits. When he turned the key, the stained wood door opened into a beautiful secluded garden.

"This is amazing. It's like an oasis," she said. It was way better than a lot of yards she'd seen in dusty drought-ridden Los Angeles.

"Let me get some plates. Maybe we can eat outside."

"I'll help," Zoe said, torn between manners and her strong desire to curl into one of the comfortable deck chairs and wait for her problems to melt away.

She couldn't have said what she'd expected from a bus driver's house, but this was very different. It was more spare than sparse. The glass door opened onto a living/dining room. She followed him through a hall, past a worktable filled with tiny tools, to a small galley kitchen with a hodgepodge of cabinets, some slate blue, others white. Efficiently, he pulled two plates from a cupboard. Cutlery and navy blue cloth napkins came next.

The narrow galley kitchen made for tight quarters.

WANDERLUST

By Zöe Andreis

Max fiddled with the tight knot on the plastic bag holding the takeout for long seconds. Eventually he left the plastic handles untied and turned to her, his bum resting against the countertop.

"I think there's something you should know," he started.

Zoe's stomach plummeted to her toes. Had any man ever said that without something crazy behind it? She let out a breath and copied his lean against the cold white stove. "What?"

"Luis Varga died."

Relieved laughter erupted from her mouth before she could stop it. Before she could do anything about the 'did I invite a crazy person in my house' look that flitted across his handsome face.

"I know," Zoe replied, sobering. "I tried to visit him in Emergency."

"Oh. That must have been awful for you."

She only nodded. Then her throat closed. Her heart squeezed. Her eyes prickled with unshed tears. If she spoke at that moment, if she said a single word at all, the waterworks would start. That couldn't happen. That's not how dates went. She was supposed to have her best face on. Zoe had always been the funny one that told jokes, made people laugh. But the thought of trying to be funny sat like a pit in her stomach. Keeping back tears was getting harder by the moment.

Through blurred vision, she saw rather than heard Max mouth her name.

"Zoe?"

She tried to nod, but was unsuccessful at that as well. In a flash, Max was across the tiny space, pulling her into his arms. "I'm sorry you had to witness that today," he said. His warm breath whispered through her hair.

"It's not your fault," she said to his chest. "You were so calm." The pique knit of polo fabric was both rough and soft against her face.

"I'm sorry to say it's not the first time it's happened. So many people work every day, sun up to sundown. They don't take vacations, they don't rest, then they die."

"I don't want my dad to die," Zoe admitted on a whisper. She'd held that fear in for weeks. Smiling for her father. Being chipper for her brother. Making sure not to make sad faces in front of the baby. Trying so hard to keep her chin from doing that dimply thing that looked like she was holding back tears. It was such a relief to let it all go —if only for a moment.

"Sounds like he has quality care. Good people looking after him to make sure he gets what he needs. Most men couldn't ask for more."

Zoe stepped back a sliver, and looked up into those gold green eyes. By degrees, her grief was replaced with something far different. Warmth spread from her core outward. She could have no more kept her hands from wrapping around his neck and tangling in his hair than she could have stopped breathing. She didn't know whose mouth moved first, his or hers. One second they were a hair's breadth apart, and the next their mouths were fused.

Sterile hospital rooms and the wailing sounds of fire-fighters' sirens swept from her mind on a wave of lust. It rose like the Pacific at high tide, quickly, unexpectedly, totally taking over. Max's mouth, tentative at first, slanted across hers, sweeping the beginning of the day, the anxiety of the last few weeks away like the ocean swept driftwood into the sea.

Zoe's entire body vibrated with the need to be consumed. Throwing modesty to the wind, she opened to him. She swept her tongue across his lips and into his mouth. Licorice or anise or something spicy sweet greeted her. She wanted more. So much more.

The erection pressing against her waist told her that Max needed this too. This release from all that had been bad and scary during the day.

Unlacing her fingers from his neck, she slipped down the rough-smooth pique fabric of his shirt, molding her fingers against his muscles along the way. She picked her way through his belt loops until she got to the snap in front. A single pop and it opened.

"Zoe." Max pulled back. The swish of cold air that went with his retreat was the last thing that she wanted touching her skin.

"What do you need Max?"

"Reassurance. Tell me I'm not taking advantage."

"No. Never. I need this with you. Here. Now," she whispered, laying herself bare.

Max jerked a thumb to the right. Without a word, she used her palms to push herself from the stove. The cold metal burned her body like fire. She followed for a few steps. Late afternoon sun streamed through the windows. Dust sparkled, suspended in the air. The gold and brown and gray and blue striped duvet on the king sized bed only a few feet past the kitchen called to her like a beacon. She kicked off first one canvas sneaker, then the other inside the door. Wiggling her bare toes against the pickled wood floor, Zoe took a deep breath. Lifting her head, then her lashes, she looked at the man filling the room.

Yes.

She wanted this.

Now.

With him.

After taking two strides toward the bed, she pulled him in for another kiss. Magic like the first time. Damn.

There was no air in the room. Pulling back to take in

much needed oxygen, Zoe snatched her T-shirt over her head, shucked her skirt.

"Jesus," Max said on an inhale.

"I know," Zoe replied. She did know. She couldn't remember the last time she'd felt anything like this hunger. Sliding her arms under his shirt, she gripped the hard muscles of his back, molded his sides, walked her fingers through the light dusting of hair, brushing his tiny nipples along the way. It was too much and too little at the same time. She wanted to see. She whisked the shirt up and over. Damn. Acres of skin begged for her lips, mouth, tongue. Just a tiny taste, she promised herself as she licked through the whorl of hair surrounding his tiny brown nipple. Yes…he tasted as good as he looked.

"I want to taste you too," Max rasped on an exhale.

In response, she unhooked her bra. Max kneeled and skimmed off leggings and panties, leaving her bare.

His big hands shimmied back up her body, making her cold and hot all at the same time. Like a well-choreographed waltz, they danced their way to the edge of the big bed. Reluctantly she let go of his arms and laid herself across the duvet.

He looked at her like she was a buffet.

She wanted to be devoured.

The single thumb he pressed into the arch of her foot nearly lifted her off the bed. The combination of pleasure and pressure hinged on sweet pain. The same strong fingers massaged and stroked her legs in equal measure. Any thoughts of restraint flew out his picture windows and she widened her legs for him, eager to receive the pleasure his touch promised.

Max didn't hesitate. He didn't disappoint. The first touch of a single finger pad nearly killed her. With the second touch of only his breath, her own breathing stopped and Zoe thought she was likely nearly dead. The third touch of his tongue, and she lost a long chunk of time. When she came to herself, Zoe wanted to crawl out of her own skin the pleasure was so pure.

Minutes transformed into tiny units of toe-curling lust. When a single thick finger joined his mouth, Zoe lost herself again. She knew the hoarse shouts were hers. Giving in, she cried, groaned and shouted through one orgasm that morphed, changed, and strung along into another.

The bed groaned in protest when Max crawled to the top. The room came into focus again and she turned her head to the side. His head rested on his hands. Elbows jutted to the side. The man had nice elbows. Geez. His smile was lazy and sexy all at the same time.

"I can barely move," she groaned.

"Then I did my job."

She fitted her hand to the golden shoulder. It was as hard and smooth as stone. But warm, so very warm. With a single finger, she tickled at the warm hair under his arm, then stroked down his flank. A perfectly muscled butt rose from back to thigh. Zoe's finger turned to a palm. Exploration made her needy again. Her push was gentle, but Max rolled over. His erection, strong, pulsing, jutted from the nest of hair at its apex. Her mouth watered.

Consume him is what she wanted to do. Lethargy battled with lust. She grasped him in her hand. Slowly up, slowly down she stroked the shaft.

"Do you have a condom?"

Unwinding her fingers from his shaft, Max rolled away from her, pawing through a side drawer. She was rewarded with a black foil packet and the return of full frontal nudity.

"Let me," Zoe said, took the rubber out and smoothed it down his length.

His eyes, heavy lidded with arousal, didn't leave hers. By degrees, each of them moved closer until their lips came together. It was so freaking hot, she thought she'd explode. The sounds he uttered in the back of his throat made her squeeze her thighs together. At the same moment she gripped him in her fist, his roughened finger brushed one nipple, then the other. Her belly dipped, her thighs slick in anticipation rubbed together. Closer they inched until they were face to face. He lifted her leg over his hip. One second, cool air brushed against her sex. In the next, he notched against her. Breaking their kiss, he whispered, "This okay?"

"More than okay," she pushed out against her stuttering heart.

Slowly he filled her.

So slow.

So full.

His movements were measured. Her arousal built slowly this time. Like the insides of a watch, the spring turned tighter and tighter.

"Oh, God," she cried. "Max, I have to…I need to…I'm going to—"

A single finger lifted her chin. Her eyes flew open. His gold green ones impaled her. Held her still for a long second. Then the wave crested over her and she was a goner. He thrust into her faster as her orgasm peaked.

Max was moving, but his chest wasn't. Why was he holding back?

"Breathe. Let go," she said. His eyes closed, breaking their intense stare. Smooth strokes gave way to jerky movements until his hoarse shout bounced off the white walls, and all movement came to a halt.

Down they came together. Zoe didn't know how long they stayed joined. But she tried not to feel bereft when Max did what was necessary.

Without words, they spooned. She faced the windows. The shadows grew long as the sunshine gave way to moonlight. Max's arm grew heavier on her waist, then grew slack. His breathing deepened.

The sex had emptied her mind for long blissful moments, but thoughts slammed her again. Zoe had never been a sex-with-a-stranger kind of girl. Well, not in the last few years at least. Up until a few minutes ago, hook-up culture had sort of passed her by. Thoughts about random hookups morphed into sadness about Luis Varga's death, then her dad. She needed to do something that wasn't dwelling on all that was wrong in her life. The light snoring made her think Max didn't have it in him for an instant rematch, so she lifted his arm from her waist and slipped from the bed. After she pulled her T-shirt over her head and stepped back into her panties, she retrieved her backpack from where she'd dropped it by the door.

Zoe rummaged through the bag, retrieving her small sketchpad and a few charcoal pencils.

Padding back through the small house, she peered at

his work desk. Tiny tools and diagrams of watches filled the surface. A cabinet displaying a few watches lined a shelf on the wall. Watches? She hadn't seen that many precision timepieces outside of Switzerland.

Curbing her impulse to snoop any more, she padded through the kitchen and back to the bedroom. Curling up on the window seat she hadn't seen the first time she came into the bedroom, Zoe began to sketch absentmindedly. The scratch of the charcoal against the grain of the paper pulled her into that Zen place she'd loved since she could hold a pencil. Worry about Dominic and sadness about the passenger she'd met moments before his death tucked themselves into a corner of her mind.

FOUR

Max

Max woke to the sound of scratching. For a long moment he lay with his eyes closed, trying to guess what kind of critter was in the crawl space under his house. He'd had to trap and move out a family of raccoons last year. The ten gauge mesh he'd installed was supposed to keep them out. At least that was what the guy at the hardware store had promised. He'd asked his father for advice, but it hadn't been one of his good days, so he'd had to rely on the help of a stranger. Didn't yet know how that was going to work out.

He took a deep breath. The smell of something musky filled his nose. Perfume and sex. Not rodent. His eyes popped open. The mystery of the scratching was quickly solved by careful observation. Zoe was writing or drawing on a pad on her knees. Bare knees. With her mind focused somewhere else, he looked at her.

If his cock twitch was any indicator, not his type was suddenly very much his type. Her little boy shorts left acres of tanned leg exposed. The peach shirt pulled tight across her breasts. Those had been the stuff of fantasies turned to reality. His fingers itched to lift her shirt, tease her nipples into hard peaks, then taste...

Zoe's head tilted up slightly, peering at some part of him.

"Why the..." Max squinted his eyes to get a better look at her shirt, "Wanderlust T-shirts?"

"They're free," Zoe said. Her answer was oddly measured.

"Because..."

She flicked her finger at a squiggly black signature under her left nipple. Max tried to push out thoughts about her naked flesh and concentrate on the answers to the questions he'd asked.

"I couldn't opt out of the merchandising part of the syndicate agreement. So I picked T-shirts. They seemed less commercial than stuffed animals."

Merchandising. Syndicates. Probably like every other guy on the planet, a good orgasm had zapped his brain. Maybe he needed food.

"You want to try dinner now?"

Zoe carefully laid pad and pencil down on the cushion and stretched her long legs. "Sure."

He waited until she was through the bedroom door before sitting up. Pulling his underwear over his cock, stubbornly at half-mast required a lot of stretching and positioning. He was standing in the middle of the room trying to think of the best way to solve his dilemma when Zoe leaned her head between the door and jamb. "Where are the—"

Her eyes dropped to his hands. The blood rushed from his head back to his cock, reversing the mental work he'd done for the last minute.

"You need help with that," Zoe said, advancing on him.

The safe haven of food and kitchens and clothed people at tables slipped from his mental grasp.

"We should talk," he said, grabbing for a lifeline.

"About what you'd like me to do to your cock?" She tilted her head like she was considering many options. He liked options.

"I'm not asking for anything," he was careful to say.

"Why not? Don't you want me to…hmm… touch…taste?"

"Oh, God. Of course I want that. But I can't—"

"Yes. You can. I want nothing more than to take you….You know what. This is too much talking," she said.

Long golden limbs attached to a very hot woman climbed up his bed.

His bed.

He had a sense that if he blinked she would disappear. So he didn't blink. He watched. Tush in the air, she stacked and fluffed a few pillows together. Max pushed his hand against his underwear, holding himself back. He wanted to lunge and take in all of this woman. If he took what he wanted, that would be too much for her. So he watched some more.

And waited.

And wanted.

Zoe took her sweet time making herself very comfortable. She lay on her back, head and breasts elevated—

nearly all his pillows underneath. Her feet were flat on the covers. Her thighs fell open.

He nearly fell over.

"Come here Max," she beckoned.

"Where?" he croaked out, walking to the edge of the mattress.

"Straddle me," Zoe commanded.

He'd never get that close without exploding. His head swam with arousal. The blood was leaving his head rapidly—again. "How?"

Zoe took each of his hands. He let her lead him closer and closer to those green eyes—smiling lips. Chest rising and lowering with her breath. He followed until his knees were on either side of the peach cartoon shirt.

"Crap. I did this all wrong. Stand up," she said.

Unable to form a clear thought, Max followed her lead.

"Take off those shorts, then come back down."

How in the hell was she keeping her voice level? She sounded like a God damn phone operator; all smooth even tones. He knelt again, conscious of how hard he was, how he was vibrating like a divining rod.

"Can you push up my shirt?"

Of course he could. But could he not bust his nut in the next forty-five seconds; that would be the true test of endurance. He eased up the soft peach cotton. He couldn't resist laying a flat palm against each orb. Hard nipples tickled his flesh and made his cock all the harder. Move, that's what he wanted to do. Because he couldn't stop himself, he pushed his cock along the smooth skin between her breasts.

Once.

Twice.

The friction did nothing to ease the sweet pain. Closing his eyes, he took in deep gulps of air.

"Jesus. Fuck," he cried out when the warmth of her mouth enveloped him. One lick turned to two. A flat tongue against the sensitive underside of his dick morphed into a suck. He tried to hold himself back, but her strong fingers pulling his butt forward spurred him on. When he'd gotten up this morning, he'd been hoping to see Zoe, get a smile and maybe her number. A blowjob had not entered his mind, was never in the picture, but here he was with her warm mouth pulling the life out of him.

Zoe let him go. He started to rear back to get another condom because he needed to bury himself deep.

"Don't move," she said. Pushing her small breasts together, she created a tunnel. "Push down." Lightly, he held his penis down. It was hell holding his hips steady. He sought relief with one or two thrusts.

"That's it exactly. Move."

With her permission, Max plowed back and forth. It was so good. So damned good. He tried to pull up, but she gripped him harder.

"Damn it Zoe, I'm going to come," he ground out, trying to hold back the inevitable.

"I sure as shit hope so," she said. Her voice had gone all hoarse and husky. That little bit of gravel in her voice was all it took. Like a fire hose relieved of pressure, he came all over her chest. Contrition restricted his breathing.

"I'm sorry," he said.

"I'm not." She tapped his leg and he lifted. Zoe lifted the shirt and tossed it on the floor. Her panties followed. Max held his dick in his hand while she strode across his bedroom. Next he knew, the shower was running. Of course, the thing about living in a bungalow the size of a tiny apartment was that there was only a single bathroom.

Two minutes later, he gave up sitting on the bed holding himself and walked into the small bathroom. Shower curtains weren't sexy. Why hadn't he seen that before? Shower curtains were Norman Bates and dysfunctional mothers. He couldn't remember a movie where the couple got it on in the steamy confines of an anti-bacterial plastic sheet.

"Zoe?" he asked. "Okay if I come in?"

He couldn't quite make out her muffled response.

"I need to clean up and I only have the one bathroom," he said. Heat rose in his face. If she asked, he'd chalk it up to all the steam. This was the hard part. Where sex went from hot to awkward.

No response.

"Zoe?"

He ducked his head around the curtain. The sexy confident Zoe of minutes ago had vanished. In her place was a woman curled into a ball. Her body wracked with sobs.

Max didn't hesitate. He stepped into the spray and gathered her in his arms. "Jesus. I'm sorry. What did I do?" Guilt at taking pleasure without reciprocation filled his belly, pushing out lust and hunger. "You didn't have to.... God this is why...."

Zoe's head snapped up. She wiped tears from her eyes.

Then she laughed. Droplets of water streamed through her short dark hair and down her face.

"I'm confused," he said. Ten years ago, he'd have tried to be what he thought was suave and sophisticated and act like he could read her mind. But not anymore. He'd learned that women were hard enough to understand. So he asked what they meant. "You don't think what we did back there…that I debased you or anything."

"That? No, I loved making you come like that." But the little hitch in her voice, even huskier from crying, said something was wrong.

"Then what is it?"

"My dad might die. I hate Los Angeles," she said in the most confusing non-sequitur ever.

"Why do you hate Los Angeles?" he asked, tackling the easiest of the questions.

"I don't have a car."

Max smoothed down a small brown spike of hair that was defying gravity and water and pointing straight to the ceiling. "I'm glad you took the bus."

"Can we turn off the water? I feel ridiculous sitting like this. If it were some silly Hollywood picture, I'd be doing this fully dressed. But this isn't some movie."

Max stood and shut the taps. "Give me a second." He pulled a towel from the bar and stepped out. Plundering through the linen cabinet, he pulled a plush terrycloth robe. The gilt-edged maroon garment had been a gift from his mother. Guilt had kept him from throwing it away.

"Put this on," he said, easing back the white plastic curtain.

"This is nice," she said, stepping into it. He wrapped it

tight and knotted the belt around her small waist. It was a little big in the chest, but didn't hang past her hands or drag on the floor.

"Why don't you get comfortable on the bed? I'll get us the food," he said.

By rote, he stuck first one container, then another in the microwave. Pulling a tray from a cabinet, he piled everything on it, got the forks and napkins from earlier.

"What do you like best?" he asked, laying the tray flat on the duvet. The sudden air on his ass and a short bark of a laugh told him he'd offered more than food.

"That..." Zoe raised her eyebrows suggestively, "wasn't too bad."

"Damn," he muttered. He pulled on his boxers for the third time that day.

"Do you want some *mics*?" She speared the little flavored meatball and held it above his plate.

"You first," he said. He watched her get a little of everything: meat, pickles, cheese.

"What's your favorite Hungarian food?"

Zoe chewed thoughtfully. *"Liba máj lilahagymalekvárral."*

"You like goose liver paté?"

"Who wouldn't? I really like that red onion jam, though. If I'd known I'd be here so long, I'd have smuggled some past customs."

"Maybe I can make it for you," he said, gathering the loose threads of thought and knitting them back together. He was sure he'd seen his mother make it in the early fall with vegetables from the old roadside markets.

"You know how?"

He nodded. "There's a secret to it."

"What?" Zoe asked. She leaned forward. The bathrobe gaped. He studiously avoided looking between the gold braid edged lapels.

"Wine."

"Seriously? There's wine in there?"

"It's the main ingredient in the fruit soup too."

She leaned back, licking something from her fork. "Damn. I should have guessed. Ouzo was my dad's secret ingredient when he cooked." Zoe's voice cracked again. "Oh, God. Papa."

"What's wrong with him exactly?" Max asked, hoping the answer wasn't five weeks to live or something equally terminal.

"That's just it. No one has a freaking clue around here. He nearly passed out on his job in Malibu at some celebrity's house. But she's so crazy about her privacy that she refused to call an ambulance. Instead, my brother had to come down from Ventura County and instead of taking my dad to the hospital, they took him to his flat.

"Then my genius brothers sat around for a day wondering what in the hell was wrong with him. They call me in the middle of the night asking for advice. Then rush him to the hospital on my say so. The ER found nothing wrong. So Papa goes back to work for that lady. Driving too far and probably doing all the heavy lifting by himself. So it happened again in his apartment and the people upstairs at least had the brains to dial nine-one-one. Same routine. He gets there, no one can find anything wrong."

"Doesn't sound like he's on the verge of death, exactly," Max tried to reassure. He'd seen the brink of death. He'd seen death. This didn't sound like it.

"But what if it's some silent killer? Mini strokes or something. Then a big attack will come and take him down."

"He sounds like he's getting good care though. He's being monitored at least."

"Maybe." She raised a single shoulder in a helpless shrug. "I don't know."

"Where is he now?"

"At my brother's place," she answered. Zoe placed her fork and napkin on the tray. Sat back, crossing her arms.

"In Ventura?"

"No. A different brother. He lives in Beverly Hills."

At least she wasn't alone. He knew what alone with illness and medical professionals was like. He didn't wish that on anyone. But he didn't want to go down that road, not with her, not in his mind either. He changed the subject to the thing that had woken him up what seemed like hours ago.

"What were you doing by the window?"

Zoe scrunched up her face. Before the really good boob job, he wanted to prompt, but didn't. "Oh, on the pad? Sketching," she answered like everyone everyday took charcoal to paper while sitting half naked in his bedroom.

"What?"

She pursed her lips in such a way that he knew, despite his lack of mind reading abilities, she was making up her mind about something.

"I'll show you," she said and moved to retrieve the

paper from the cushion. Max took the spiral pad thrust at him. It was him, sleeping. Even though it was black and white, it was so true-to-life, he felt like he could reach through the paper and touch the man laying between the rumpled sheets.

"This is good. Do you do this for a hobby?" he asked, thinking of his own tinkering with watches.

"Yes, I sketch for fun. But I draw for a living."

"Draw?"

Zoe retrieved the shirt from the floor and shook it out. He looked at the cartoon again a lot more closely this time. It was a four-panel cartoon with a woman holding a map.

"Wanderlust?" he asked. It was the title on the upper left.

"It's my strip."

"You draw a comic strip? In the papers?"

"For the last five years, yep."

"What's it about?"

"Wanderlust. I live in a different city every year or so, then write about the humor in cultural interpretation."

"That's cool," he said, feeling positively provincial. Driving the same route ten times a day wasn't exactly globe-trotting. "So you're writing about Budapest now?"

"I haven't written a thing for the last four weeks that I've been here. And I'm not experiencing the cultural divide because I'm not in a different culture. Well, that's not true, but no one wants to read about L.A.," she said, sounding like she'd rather be anywhere but Los Angeles. He wanted to say there was plenty dividing the different communities in L.A. He saw it every day on the bus. But she hadn't come to his house for a debate.

"Are you done?" he asked.

"With the food, yes. With you, no," Zoe said.

She was going to kill him. He'd never known someone so forward and honest with their sexuality. Her words hit him in all the right places, head, heart, down low.

Max came back to bed, wanting answers to so many questions in his mind. He started with one.

"Where were you before Hungary?"

"Guess you're not one of my readers," she said, her smile slow to come. "Athens. Prague. Dublin. Milan. Now Budapest. I'm thinking Krakow next."

"Not Los Angeles," he said, wondering why the fact that someone he didn't know wasn't staying in California disappointed him so much.

"My main audience is American. So I don't think that would work. But enough about that. Let's go to bed."

"I don't think."

"Don't," she said, pulling him closer. "We did this totally backwards."

Her lips touched his lightly, brushing back and forth. The friction zapped him everywhere. His skin pulled tight. Max could have sworn every follicle on his skin was raised in gooseflesh. A hand sifted through the strands of his hair, along his jaw, neck, collarbone before landing on the spot between his back and butt. God, it was so good just kissing Zoe. Between the dart of her tongue between his lips, opening to accept her exploration and demand his own, he tried to remember if they'd kissed before.

When she pulled back a bit, a space opening between them, he looked at her. The short dark hair that framed her face. Strong cheekbones and full lips. Green, green eyes. He ran a finger between the voluminous folds of the bathrobe, slipping between them to take the slight weight of a single breast into his palm. Rasping first his palm, then finger across the nipple, the sound of Zoe's gasp filled the room.

The twitching down below was only a half-salute. "I can't, but do you want me to—"

Zoe shrugged a single shoulder from the robe. It fell open and she lay on it like a Greek goddess, which was the least ironic thing in the world.

"You look like *Venus at her Mirror*," he said.

"Velázquez's nude? At the National Gallery?" He couldn't help but detect the surprise in her voice.

"I get off the bus once in a while," he said, unable to keep the laugh from his voice.

"I didn't mean…It's just London. Damn it. Kiss me again. I really like doing that with you."

He needed no further invitation to lean in close and take her lips.

♥

MAYBE ONE OTHER time in his life, when he was fifteen or so, had he done nothing but kiss for hours. But that's what they'd done. At least that's the best of his memory. Because at some point he must have fallen asleep, between kissing and talking and more kissing. The noise that brought him to wakefulness wasn't scratching this time, but the sound of wind. When he closed his eyes and thought of it, he realized it wasn't wind, but rain. He sat up to say something to Zoe about the rarity of it, but he was surprised to find himself alone. The robe was folded neatly on the window seat. The sound of something crinkling had him lifting his hand. In the faint light, he could see a thick sheet of paper. He picked it up to examine it more closely. It was a cartoon.

Zoe Andreis, it was signed. He squinted to read the words scrawled below: Thanks for helping me forget.

His heart pounded in his chest and his stomach roiled in protest. Forget? Forget what? There was no way he was ready to forget what had to be one of the best nights of his life. The paper fluttered to the floor as Max fell back on the bed. Was he someone Zoe didn't want to remember?

FIVE

Zoe

The only thing worse than the relentless sun of Los Angeles: the threat of rain. The driver in the car share had nearly run off the road when it had started sprinkling. He spent another ten of the fifteen-minute drive trying to get the wipers to work. Zoe looked at the receipt on her phone. She could have gone the bus route and saved twenty bucks. Maybe she'd have met another cute bus driver.

Nope she wouldn't go there. One bus driver was enough.

Grateful to be in her own tiny bungalow safe and nearly dry, she tossed off the clothes she'd put on and off a zillion times in the last twenty-four hours. She showered and tried to push the previous night from her mind.

But the cold hard facts of what she'd done wouldn't leave her.

She'd had sex with a near stranger. Layer on top of that her looming deadlines and her sick dad, and she wanted nothing more than to get into bed again…alone. But Nicki's text had launched her out of Max Kiss' bed, into the car, and back here. There wasn't any hiding from the cold hard facts now.

Her phone buzzed against the pencil ledge of the cheap drafting desk she'd bought secondhand. Instead of tossing the phone out the window like she wanted, Zoe picked it up and started at the green text bubble.

"Where are you?" Nick.

"What's up?" she texted back though she knew damn well what was up. Her dad wanted to have some kind of serious talk with her and her brother. More than once in her childhood, her father had mock threatened her and her brothers with certain death for their bad behavior. His threat hadn't sounded as fake this time around. She wanted to avoid certain death more than she wanted to avoid the sick man.

"Dad wants you," Nicki replied. Zoe resisted the urge to type: no shit Sherlock.

"Is he dying?" she typed, only half kidding. Half wanting to be prepared for the worst.

"He's fine. Waiting for you."

"Be there in twenty." She pressed send, then typed again. "Make that thirty. Rain makes Angelenos crazy."

Thirty-five frustrating minutes later, she knocked on her brother's door. No answer. She pounded again. She hadn't brought a raincoat and was getting soaked in the desert downpour. The driver who'd taken her up Nicki's pothole pocked street had been eager to get on to the next fare. He hadn't been interested in making sure she got in safe and dry.

"Sorry," Holly said when she finally opened the door. The pretty curly haired fiancé of her brother was holding their baby, Iris. "She was crying. Nick dropped her diaper, face down. Dominic…Oh…sorry, you're dripping wet. Come in. Nick!" she called. "Bring your sister a towel."

"Must be great to have short hair. Dries super quick," said the spirally bouncy curly haired fiancé.

"Makes travel easy," she grumbled. Plucking the T-shirt away from her chest saved her from saying anything to Holly. The woman seemed lovely. But the mommy, earth mother routine rubbed her a little bit the wrong way.

"Do you want to hold your niece?" Holly said, her smile positively beatific. If Max were here, he'd probably point out her soon-to-be sister in law's resemblance to Bottecelli's portraits of young women, all rosy cheeked and flowing hair.

Had Max been to the Uffizi gallery? Holly's voice swept away the fantasy of her walking hand in hand with him through cool museum corridors.

Holly held the dark haired child out to her. Iris was sucking her hand with a profusion of drool. Zoe didn't want to get any damper than she already was. Trying not to visibly recoil, she said, "I'm good. Babies don't like me." Tiny human beings were so not her thing.

Thankfully her brother appeared with the towel. Grabbing at it with both hands mooted the baby holding question.

"Where's Papa?" Zoe asked, rubbing the flowery smelling towel through her nearly dry hair. She'd always been the Andreis sibling who stood still and took her medicine, who ate her vegetables first, and came whenever their dad called.

A look passed between Holly and Nicki. This wasn't a parenting emergency look, or a smoldering sex look. She'd seen both of those. This was guilt, plain and simple. Her brother hesitated about five beats too long.

"He's not in bed, is he?" Zoe said, marching purposefully up the steps from the tiny vestibule. "Papa?" she called, scoping out the living room, empty save for some foam blocks and kid toys. "Papa!" she yelled into the little kitchen alcove. Nothing. She trooped up some more narrow stairs to the third story and called out again.

"Out here!" he answered back.

Zoe yanked back the curtains along the back wall of a bedroom covering one of the four French doors. With the towel in her hand, she rubbed vigorously at the condensation obscuring her view of the little patio behind the house.

Legs on a tall stepstool was all she could see. She wrestled with the brass door handle until the seal gave and the door flew open.

"What are you doing? On a ladder? In the rain?" When he didn't answer, she tried again. "Papa? Answer me."

"I saw a damp spot on the wall so I came to clear out this gutter. No big deal," her father answered. Five seconds later, a thick bundle of smelly, rotting leaves splatted by her feet. Brown bits of leaf matter stuck to her bare calves.

"You're supposed to be resting," she said, holding out her hand to help her dad down the ladder.

"It's all done," he said, brushing his hands together, then rubbing them against ancient looking jeans.

"Nicki could have done that, Papa."

"He was in the middle of a diaper explosion." Dominic shrugged. "Had to pick my poison, so I chose this."

"There are two full grown adults downstairs. I saw them with my own eyes. They should be able to take care of a single human being who can't weigh more than twenty pounds."

"Says the woman with no babies. You try cleaning up a poopy, squirrely, eighteen month old."

"Fine. Whatever. I'm not here to argue with you. Come inside."

Dominic stepped into the house, careful not to track mud from his boots. "It was no big deal, Zoe. Just some leaves. You are overreacting."

Her dad listed a little to the right trying to pull off work boots.

"Sit. I'll help."

Dominic sat on a steamer trunk that had to be older than her, her dad, and the house combined. "Where does Holly get this stuff?" she asked while unlacing first one boot, then the second.

"Nice, huh?" her dad asked rhetorically while easing off the thick leather. Nice isn't the word she'd have used to describe the decades old brass studded box. Zoe caught the boots and nearly fell on her ass.

"How in the hell much do these weigh?"

"Don't know. Maybe four or five pounds each. Been thinking maybe I don't so much need them anymore.

Adonis was wearing some red bird, feather, no...red wing boots that looked nice."

"Nicki can take you to the shoe store," Zoe said, standing and looking anywhere but at her father.

"You still can't forgive him, can you?"

"I don't know what you're talking about," Zoe said, trying to swallow the bile rising in her throat. She opened the French door and used her hands to scrape off the wet sand caked into the seam of the boots. Her father had always prided himself on keeping his boots and tools oiled and in top condition.

In his socks, her father didn't walk any farther than the sliding door track that rose from the floor, but she could practically feel his breath on her neck.

"What?"

"I have a dying wish."

"Ten seconds ago, you were fine, Papa." Zoe stopped speaking before her voice could break. She wouldn't burden her dad with the unmistakable sense of futility pulsing through her veins.

"Listen to me. I don't know what's wrong. I could live another thirty years. I could live another three days. But either way. I gotta get this off my chest."

"If you start the 'one family' lecture, I'm bailing."

"You only get one family," Dominic started anyway. "I love each and every one of you as much as a father could love a child. Your mom is already gone. When I go, you'll only have your brothers."

Zoe couldn't prevent the teenaged style huff that left her lips.

Dominic ignored her like he'd done all those years ago

when her fourteen-year-old self had adopted the same posture.

"You need to forgive him."

"What are you, Oprah? He doesn't deserve forgiveness. Here." She thrust the boots at her dad and stepped past him into the room. "The rest of this mud will be easier to get off when it dries."

"Where are you going?" Dominic called to her back.

"You're alive. I can't blow my deadlines anymore. Outta here. Call me if there's an emergency."

"You haven't seen me in three years and all I get to see is your back?"

"That's low for you, Papa. You were never one to do the guilt thing."

"You don't have a mama anymore. Someone's got to do it."

"Do you have something wrong with your brain? You never talk about Mama that way. God rest her soul," Zoe said, doing the sign of the cross.

"Ah Jesus," Dominic said. He sank back into a tufted pink floral armchair that would have swallowed a lesser man. "Sorry. Iris loved you guys. It would have killed her to see this rift between you and your brother."

"Bad choice of words all around."

"Sorry about that."

"How are you feeling, Papa? For real?"

"Scared, Zoe."

She grabbed his hand. It was cold from working outside without gloves. She rubbed it between hers, trying to make them warm. She turned her father's hand over. It wasn't nearly as rough as she remembered. It was big and square, though. A masculine version of her own.

"Those damned doctors. Maybe I need to take a trip over to UCLA and make arrangements for a third opinion."

"I feel okay right now. Need a break from doctors. Want to get that house done."

"With the woman who wouldn't call the doctor?"

"Gemma."

"What's her story? Was she going to let you die on her front lawn because she's afraid of men with telephoto lenses?"

"You're playing the blame game, Zoe."

"Am I wrong? You can't get a diagnosis. The woman you're working for doesn't believe in nine-one-one. And my dear oldest brother…let's not even go there."

"This negativity is going to kill you."

"Ah jeez. You sound like some California hippie. All of you have been out here way too long. Sometimes bad things happen, Papa. I don't want them to happen to you. I can't rely on warm light or healing vibes, or any of that to help you out. Western medicine can work."

"I'm not exactly sitting on the floor in an orange robe chanting Om, Zoe."

"You might as well be. The only thing between you and some kind of diagnosis is obstinance or insurance. Nobody here seems to be managing either. I'll move heaven and earth to get that crap out of the way and get you well."

"I may sound hippie dippie. But you sound European."

"Single payer healthcare isn't the worst thing to happen to a civilized society."

"Medicare *is* single payer."

"At thirty five dollars a pop or whatever for doctor visits, I don't think you're getting the absolute best care."

"Give it…" Dominic gasped for air. He lifted his arms toward the heavens. "I'm coming to join you, Iris."

Her father clutched his chest in the best imitation of Red Foxx she'd ever seen. At least she hoped it was a joke.

"You okay?" she asked with her tongue firmly planted in cheek.

"Talk to your brother," Dominic ordered. His tone was normal. No gasping, no clutching, all seriousness.

"I'll think about it," was her grudging reply.

"Fine. I smell lunch. Let's see what Holly's got on the table. She's a great cook."

Zoe rolled her eyes as dramatically as she could muster. "I don't think Nicki plans to marry her for her cooking."

"He's going to marry her because she got knocked up." Dominic practically skipped down the stairs, eager for a meal. He'd always liked good food.

Zoe giggled. She never giggled. Then she let it out. Tears poured down her cheeks. But if it was because of grief or love or humor, she didn't know.

Lunch looked like it was going to be lentil soup, homemade bread, and baby spit up. Zoe was careful to take a seat at the refectory table far from the toddler banging on her plastic tablemat.

"Too bad you missed dinner last night. Holly made

pastitsio," Dominic said. He tucked his napkin into his shirt and made no effort to slurp his soup silently.

"That's my favorite," Zoe said. The sudden ache in her chest was a reminder of her mom and dad's regular fight in the kitchen over the proper ingredients for cooking. Mom had called it Greek lasagna. She'd snuck in marinara sauce and omitted other stuff she'd said was too Greek.

"She always left out the cinnamon," her dad said, his thoughts paralleling hers.

Zoe looked anywhere but at the three adults and one child sitting at the table. Crying wasn't something she did. And if she did cry, it was something she never did in front of anyone else, last night being the one glaring exception.

"Where were you last night anyway?" Nicki asked. "We texted you a bunch of times."

The truth and a lie were holding equal space in her head. But Max's penis and cartoon strips took up so much room in her brain that her speech center was rendered mute. Didn't stop her heart from pumping blood up to her face, though. Heat swirled around her.

"Are you blushing?" Nicki asked, pointing a finger at her.

Leave it to your siblings to be failingly honest and direct.

"No, I'm not blushing," Zoe said. "I don't blush." She picked up her spoon and swirled some kind of creamy garnish into the orange puree.

"If you're not embarrassed, answer the question," Nicki said.

"I was on a date," she said before guilt flooded her veins and cut off speech. Because dating and sick dad didn't mix. "I mean, you said you were okay to be here, Papa, and when this guy I met called, I didn't think it would be bad to go to dinner. It was Hungarian food. He's Hungarian...." Zoe stopped talking because all eyes were on her. Even Iris had stopped banging and smearing. The little girl with her own mother Iris' eyes was looking at her intently.

Dominic clapped his hands. "Maybe one of my kids will actually get married!"

"We're engaged, Dad," Nicki said.

"You move too damn slow," Dominic said.

"It's just that we haven't set a date," Nicki said.

"Sap runs from a maple tree faster than you get anything done."

"Not as fast as they had a baby," Zoe huffed.

"That's not fair. The documentary just wrapped up. Holly wants Iris to be able to walk down the aisle with us. We don't know where we want to get married. Planning a wedding isn't as easy as saying 'I do," Nicki explained.

Zoe watched the back and forth, glad to be out of the limelight. But her brother was a smart cookie. He moved a water glass out of his daughter's reach while at the same time, he zeroed back in on her.

"Who's the guy? You've been in town five minutes. How did you meet someone?"

Little tidbits. If she gave them those, she hoped they'd lay off her. What had happened between Max seemed like a fever dream. But the kind of dream a woman kept to herself.

"His name is Max," she said, dropping his name like Hansel and Gretel would drop a crumb.

"Where did you meet him?" Holly asked.

"On the bus," Zoe hedged. She didn't know why it felt like a secret, but she didn't reveal more.

"Long ride?" Holly asked. She got up from her half eaten soup and lifted Iris from her chair. The child latched on to her mother's hip like Velcro. With a child in hand, Zoe assumed no double entendre was meant even if her own mind had dropped straight into the gutter.

"Saw him on there a couple of times. Figured there was no harm in giving him my number."

"You want to invite him over for dinner? I'm sure Holly's got something good in the oven," Dominic said, lifting his nose to the air like a scenting bloodhound.

"Another baby?" Zoe asked under her breath.

"Country style ribs," Nicki's fiancée said like it was a restaurant.

"Sounds all well and good, but I really do have to get back to the drawing board."

"Ha, that's funny, sis. Maybe you should put it in a strip."

SIX

Max

Max picked up and dropped the tiny tools about twenty times before he haphazardly shoved them all in their box. Swiveling around in his chair, he retrieved his laptop from the antique secretary he'd inherited.

The hulking furniture in his house was beautiful. No one could fault his Hungarian ancestors for their woodworking skills. But he was loath to take a saw to it, carving out the holes necessary for the cables that were the norm in today's electronically connected world. So he took the computer and its power pack outside to the little wood table. Maybe some fresh air would clear his mind of thoughts of Zoe. Two weeks ago he'd have deconstructed that watch by now, carefully labeling all the pieces, making meticulous notes about how he would proceed to repair, or figuring out if it was a lost cause. Not today, though. His concentration was shot.

Resigned, he propped open the lid. Max's fingers plunked at the keys. He'd never learned to type and despite his dexterity with the innards of watches, his hands were too big for the tiny plastic squares. He didn't know what he was looking for until his hands clicked out the words: Wanderlust.

Two clicks later, the cartoon strip that had graced Zoe's...chest...was on the front page. It was kind of funny now that he thought about it. There was a link to a page that promised today's strip. He clicked on it. A new window opened.

WANDERLUST

By Zöe Andreis

He looked at the tiny pictures. Had she drawn these or did they use computers nowadays? Had the hands that had held his cock tight also made the words above the little black and white heads? Speaking of cocks, Max chanced a look into his lap. His was coming right to attention under his gray sweats. He swiped over to the about page. Smiling back at him was Zoe, the short hair he'd seen spiky after the shower, the eyes that had gone from green to nearly black when she'd been close to orgasm, the mouth she'd encouraged him to plunge into until she sucked him dry. Embarrassed, he clicked away. His brain had turned a headshot indecent.

Slamming the metal top shut, Max hauled the computer and its cords through the bedroom doors, back into the house, and laid it back on the well-oiled wood furniture. That little frolic and detour had done nothing to turn his thoughts back to his work at hand. Patek Philippe was a new brand for him. He should be figuring out its peculiarities and not mooning around the house like a fifteen-year-old boy with a permanent hard on.

The fact that had him out of sorts was that Zoe hadn't called. In the week since she'd walked out of his little house, his phone hadn't rang once. Well, maybe once or twice. But a call from the tree trimmer to schedule his twice-yearly maintenance, and someone trying to sell him solar panels, surely didn't count.

He picked up the small phone and pressed the home button. It made one of those well-orchestrated corporate noises. A blue screen lit up. In a glance he knew the weather, the score from last night's game, and which movies were playing around the corner. He perused the screen again. Nope. Didn't say anything about whether a certain cartoonist was going to call him.

Max tossed the phone from hand to hand. Maybe he should run over to Hollywood and Highland, hit up one of those kiosks for a new case.

"Ah fuck it," he heard himself say out loud. Pulling up the number from the pocket computer's memory. He laid his finger on the glass screen. The worst she could say is no.

"Zoe Andreis." The voice that answered was efficient and businesslike. Not at all husky like when she'd been on the verge of coming for him. "Hello," she said. Max realized he'd been on the line too long without saying a thing. If he'd been a teenager in the pre-caller ID world, he'd have hung up and tried again when he'd lassoed his brain under control.

"It's Max. How's your dad?"

Her response wasn't instant. He wondered if her brain was snagging on his voice or his question.

"Good. Bad. Indifferent. I don't know. How about you?"

"Fine. Work's been good." He could have kicked himself. Who in the hell cared about his job?

"I've thought about you," she said.

His cock leapt to attention in his pants. Down boy, he wanted to mutter to it.

"That's why I'm calling. If you have some time, I thought maybe we could get together. Maybe dinner or a movie or something."

"I didn't come to Los Angeles to watch a movie, Max. But a little companionship, now that might be worth bailing on work and a family dinner for. You game?"

Zoe had made it both easier and harder. He'd wanted

the invitation. Would most definitely accept. It was hard, though, knowing what her intentions were. Before he started sounding like his father, he answered.

"Sure. What are you up for? I'm game for anything."

Her laugh was sexy, husky.

"Now that's what I like to hear." She gave him her address.

"I'll bring dinner," he promised. Then rang off.

Max hadn't known what in the hell to expect of Zoe's temporary digs. But the bungalow, shockingly smaller than his in a city of McMansions, was all art studio and bedroom. They were standing in a land of white walls and storm cloud gray bedclothes. Purposefully he walked from the bedroom back into the studio cum living room.

"You really *are* an artist," he said dumbly. Cursing himself for the implicit putdown in the statement. It's the kind of thing his own father would have said.

Zoe's eyes coolly appraised him. "It's more writing than art."

Confused, he eyed the multitude of pens, pencils, and paint brushes on her desk. "What's all that for?"

Patiently, Zoe led him through the creation of a comic strip, penciling in an idea on thick white paper, marking over that in permanent ink — the watercolor for a Sunday strip.

Trying not to break the fragile bond they'd forged, Max stepped forward and captured her wrists. "You have ink stains."

"Occupational hazard," Zoe said, looking directly into his eyes. Did she ever hide her emotions? Her thoughts.

He could see desire in her eyes, the pupils growing larger and darker with every breath.

"I brought dinner," he said, blinking and looking away. He'd dropped the bags on the counter the minute he'd walked in. The vibrant color of her Sunday cartoons and the stark black and white of the pages propped against the wall had caught his eye. Not to mention the woman in a fitted T-shirt and short shorts.

"What did you bring? I could eat a horse. Okay, maybe not a horse. Do you know they serve horse meat in Switzerland? I thought my French and German had gone to shit when I asked the restaurant servers about that. Oops, sorry. Dinner?"

WANDERLUST

By Zöe Andreis

"Is this for the cartoon?" Max asked. He picked up a picture that looked like Budapest. "Is this Parliament?"

"It's a Sunday strip. The foreground will have the girl walking along the *Duna Parton*."

The watercolor artwork was really good. His memory of reading the comics as a kid wasn't anything this evocative. "I thought strips were more Lichtenstein. But this is more John Singer Sargent."

"That's totally my influence. I mimic him because he rendered Europe in a classic way. So I'm trying to give those little glimpses of Europe to my readers."

He picked up another.

"*Hősök tere*," Zoe said.

"Hero's Square?"

He looked closer, past the nearly perfect rendering of the Seven Chieftains of the Magyars.

By Zöe Andreis

Laughter burst from him unexpectedly. "That's really funny. You totally captured the vibe there."

"Thank you," she said.

"Dinner?" he asked for a third time. She nodded.

He brought the bags to the tiny table she'd set up in a corner of the kitchen. At least she'd bought two chairs.

Zoe poked her head in a bag. "Sushi to go? Only in Los Angeles."

Max didn't think that was compliment on the versatility and diversity of a city that could render dozens of cuisines in a single square mile. "I brought sake," he said, brandishing a frosted green bottle with Japanese characters.

"We'll have to use plastic cups. Sorry. Does that ruin it?"

"All good," he said, opening the bottle and pouring an eighth of an inch in her cup. Max explained while Zoe pulled trays from the bag, "I got sashimi, the usual, tuna, yellowtail, salmon and stuff, and a bowl of *unagi*."

"I love *unagi*. Eel isn't prepared like this in Europe," Zoe said. She broke apart the bamboo chopsticks and picked up a slice of fish. Closing her eyes, she hummed in delight. Max was suddenly very glad he'd chosen fish over burritos.

"How long have you been in Europe?"

"About ten years. I left right after college graduation," she said. The wrinkle of her nose made him wonder.

"Why Europe?"

"My mom died when I was fifteen. I love my dad, but I kind of wanted to explore her family roots. I stayed in Saronno with my grandmother and great aunt. It's kind of where the comic was born."

"Is all of your family in Los Angeles?" Max asked, watching the chopsticks come to her lips again. He wanted to hold her again, kiss her like they'd done in his bedroom. But without dinner and conversation, he was nothing more than an impolite, randy teenager. "You mentioned a brother," he prompted when she didn't answer.

Zoe took a long drink of sake, then poured herself another small glass. "Damn, this is nearly as strong as *pálinka* or *ouzo*. I wonder if every culture has something this potent in the arsenal."

"Who's the brother that lives in Beverly Hills?"

"Nicki. He's younger. I have an older brother Adonis."

Max's laugh came out before he could put his hands in front of his mouth and disguise it as a cough.

"Seriously?"

"My parents weren't thinking. Or they were high. I don't know. My dad said he wanted strong Greek names for his children. So we have Adonis, Nicholas, and Zoe."

Max ate a few slices of yellowtail in silence. Taking in the idea of a big family. By the lean of her body, Max knew what question was coming next. Immediately, he regretted starting the conversation in the first damned place. He thought he'd learned better. But his curiosity about the Greek goddess who'd set his sheets on fire had overcome his normal reticence.

"You have any brothers or sisters?" Zoe asked.

The question landed like hot coals in his belly. Appetite gone, he dropped his chopsticks and pushed the black plastic tray away. His father always said he had two sons. His mother's answer was always one.

"I don't know how to answer that," he said candidly.

"Oh...kay."

"I had a brother. He died of leukemia before I was born."

"You grew up as an only child, then."

"Not exactly," he said. "It was kind of like I grew up in the shadow of a ghost."

"What was his name?"

"Jenci...Jenő."

"Do you want sake?"

Max considered the empty plastic tumbler on his side of the table. "I'll have a little," he said. Maybe it would make him less awkward. Nothing had gone quite the way he'd hoped after he'd picked up his phone. Before his finger dialed, he'd imagined dinner, a little sake, some kissing. More kissing. Maybe more than kissing. But he'd managed to insult her work and bring up the awkward topic of his brother. All before dessert. Sex, at this point, wasn't even in the vicinity.

"I brought green tea ice cream."

"Oooh. Now that sounds good," Zoe said. She gathered up the trash. "Can you take this outside? I'll get dessert ready."

Max scooped everything into the plastic take-out bag and walked where she pointed to the black trash bin.

The kitchen and living room were dark when he came back. "Zoe?"

"In the bedroom."

Three more amazing words were never spoken. He toed off his sneakers and left them by the bedroom door. Zoe was cross-legged on the duvet. "I have one bowl. Two spoons. Okay?"

He was more than okay. He walked into exactly where he wanted to be. Taking the proffered spoon, he scooped up the cool pale green cream. All done with awkwardness, he fully meant for the cool concoction to enter his mouth. But watching Zoe lick the spoon distracted him. The cold slide of liquid on his chin was the last straw. He was ready to call it a night. Go home. Hit the reset button. Try again another day. Because nothing said suave like food caught in your stubble.

"Here, let me." Zoe leaned forward and scooped the liquid from the corner of his mouth. Without pause, she licked her thumb clean. "That's even better," she said.

Better than what bubbled in his mind, but never left his mouth, because she replaced her finger with her tongue and then all thoughts scattered.

"You taste really good," she said. Her lips hovered near his for a long moment before she kissed his ear. Into it she whispered something about tasting him everywhere. But he couldn't have told a single soul what she said because the blood had already left the language processing portion of his brain for his pants.

It didn't take more than Zoe's index finger to push him back into the pillows, lending credence to the phrase knock me over with a feather. Straddling his hips, she had his shirt off in seconds.

"So I've been wondering for as long as it took to go to the trash bin if you'd let me eat this ice cream off you."

Lust had removed his vocal chords. That must have been what was wrong, because he couldn't say a word. The soft scratch of his hair against the pillows told him his head had made the wise decision to nod.

Zoe licked all the ice cream from the spoon in her hand and waved it over his body as if she couldn't decide where to start. Finally, she dipped the utensil into the bowl and scooped out a heaping spoonful. It landed on his nipple. He tried not to shiver as she took him and the confection into her mouth. The icy hot contrast nearly made him come in his pants. But she was a step ahead of him. Lifting her hips, she scooped down his pants and underwear. In the bowl, the spoon went again, a tiny wet plop landed on his belly button. Off his lap she came, and onto the bed. Leaning on hands and knees, she lapped it up like a cat with a bowl of cream.

"Too cold?" Zoe breathed against the thatch of hair below his navel.

"Too hot," he replied.

"Oh, so you don't want any more of this," she said, picking up the spoon one more time. This time the tiny scoop landed on the tip of him. The catlike licks she used to eat him up nearly drove him around the bend. There was no more ice cream, only Zoe's hot, wet, mouth. Max didn't have much rational thought left, but he wasn't going to let her do all the work this time. Turning the tables, he used all the willpower he had and pulled out of her all-too-willing mouth.

He moved the bowl to the table on his side of the bed and straddled her hips. He pulled the T-shirt over her head. The thin elastic waist shorts came off as quickly as the hot pink bikini underwear. One day he'd take the time to savor all there was to Zoe, but today wasn't that day. She'd created a need in him only she could satiate.

Retrieving the bowl, he followed her lead. Letting her lay prone, the rise and fall of her chest tempting him with the bob of her breasts. He licked the spoon and scooped up the runny remains. Pale green liquid drizzled first on one nipple then the other. A second scoop from the bowl gave him enough to fill her navel. Whether her sudden intake of breath was arousal or shock, he didn't know, but he watched the last bit of cream slide between her folds.

It was like a sexy scavenger hunt. First, he made his way through the cream on one side until he found the prize. A hard brown nipple. Striving to be fair, Max made sure to find the second. He lingered longer than the first because the breathy sounds he got every time he sucked made him just that much harder.

"Max, please," she begged.

He didn't deny her. First, he made sure her navel was clean. Then he spread her legs and took in the heady mixture of cream and Zoe. Thinking about the innards of the watch on his work desk kept him in check. Made it so he could take Zoe to the brink and push her over the edge. When her moans subsided and her breath evened, he came up to join her.

"Please tell me you have a condom," he said. He had never been a guy to carry one in his wallet or glove compartment.

Lethargy personified, Zoe took a long minute to get one from a basket on the table and hand it to him. Max sheathed himself and thought some more about the tiny cogs that turned the minute hands. Unable to resist any longer, he smoothed a hand through her hair, sifting through the short fine strands, then he traced the contours of her nose. His mouth replaced his hands. Sweet and salty greeted his tongue. Slow at first, the kissing picked up pace. Easing on top of her, he rubbed his hardness against her slick folds. What had started as gentle exploration turned into the very definition of hunger. But he wanted Zoe, not sushi.

Reluctantly Max broke his mouth from hers when she grasped his penis and notched it at her entrance. The tilt of her hips was all the invitation he needed to sink into her. He was on fire. Heat radiated from where he was buried to the hilt to the tips of his fingers. Rising onto his arms, he swept his eyes from where they were joined to her belly fluttering with breath, to her hard tipped breasts jiggling with each thrust, to her parted lips, to her eyes. They caught him. A storm of emotion raged within their depths. Something in her pulled at him. He couldn't look away, though.

The jumble of emotions from their frantic couplings that warred within him was mirrored in her eyes. Zoe closed hers and turned her head slightly to the side. She grasped his ass and wiggled her hips, increasing the friction. No amount of gears, cogs, and quartz movement could keep him from the brink. His balls tightened and his hips jerked against hers, the delicious squeezing from her inner walls dragging out the orgasm beyond what his mind could take. Easing from her, he collapsed by her side.

"Where's the bathroom?"

Zoe pointed to one of the two wood doors with oiled brass knobs. In the all white bathroom, he cleaned up. On his way out the door, he glanced at the man in the mirror. Damn. That guy had it bad for the woman in the other room. He blinked and turned away from the reflection.

Casual didn't need analysis.

She wasn't in bed when he came back. But the sounds of silverware, ceramic, and running water clued him in. Her smile was all Cheshire cat when she waltzed into the bedroom. He was jealous of the long silky robe she wore. How could he ever have thought tall women weren't sexy? His stomach twisted at the possibility that he could have looked past Zoe, searching for someone who didn't wind his watch like she did.

"Green tea ice cream is the best dessert ever," she said before sliding on top of the duvet he was tucked under.

"What's your passion?" she asked after a long moment of quiet.

"Other than being…" Damned if he was going to say something stupid about ways he'd like to please her. Ways he could make her call out his name. "What do you mean?" he asked instead of embarrassing himself.

"What thing do you enjoy doing more than anything else in the world?"

Sex with Zoe now ranked high on the list. But his brain was coming out of the fog and haze of arousal. He didn't think she was talking about sex. "I don't know. What's yours?"

Zoe cocked her head in that way she had. Not that he knew her well enough to know if she had a 'way' with anything she did. But she looked at him like she couldn't wait to hear what he wanted to say. She didn't answer, only waited.

"I fix vintage watches," he finally said in response.

"Like fix, how?" she asked, curiosity wrinkling her brow. He'd seen that look before. A hobby repairing old cars got you smiles and nods and lots of comparisons between automobiles and women. Watches got question marks.

Propping himself up on an elbow, he said, "I go to flea markets, estate sales, buy their broken watches. I see what's wrong. Most times I can get them up and running."

Her cool fingers grasped his empty wrists. "Where's…."

Max fished the watch he'd removed on his way to the bathroom from the table next to the bed. Handed it to her.

She turned on a gooseneck lamp. "Is that a leather strap?"

"Links came later."

She peered at the tiny letters under the twelve. A puff of frustration left her lips, and she eased on glasses he hadn't noticed. "This is a Cartier? I've never seen one like this."

"It's a Pasha." he said.

"A what?" she asked. He decided he liked her forehead wrinkled. It was unexpectedly cute on a woman who was stately, gorgeous, stunning, but probably hadn't ever been called cute.

"The Pasha of Marrakech commissioned this watch in the thirties for swimming," he explained.

Zoe's smile was slow. She turned the full force of it on him. It nearly knocked him for a loop. "What did the Pasha of Marrakech need to keep track of? Seems like the kind of guy who didn't have to clock in."

By Zöe Andreis

"You have a point." He laughed. A gorgeous woman who made him laugh. He had no idea whom to thank for winning the dating lottery. That sly humor was probably the kind of thing that kept readers glued to her strips.

"Anyway," he continued, "it's one of the first waterproof watches."

She turned it over. Even under the dim lighting the gold shone. "Pretty cool. Looks like something James Bond might have worn or a NASA astronaut."

"I'm no James Bond," he said. "More MacGyver."

"So, wait. You were saying that you buy watches and fix them?" she asked, handing the watch back to him.

"Yeah. Got this at the Rose Bowl Flea Market," he said, strapping the Pasha to his left wrist.

"How much did you pay?" she asked. "If you don't mind my asking."

"About eight hundred?"

"Dollars? How much would it be worth now that you got it working?" Calculation was hard while she was tucking her smooth legs next to his.

Tuning out the feel of her, he did some mental gymnastics. "I was lucky with this watch. Found another in worse condition to use for parts. The whole thing is original. Maybe three, four thousand. Possibly twice that." Since he didn't plan to sell value wasn't really important to him.

"That's quite the profit," she said before pulling off her glasses and laying them gently on the stacks of sketches that littered her bedside table. "So why do you do it?"

"Fix the watches? My dad...."

"No, drive the buses?" Zoe shook her head as if trying to comprehend something difficult.

"My job?" he asked, not quite getting it either. Everyone except the rich had to work. Maybe Zoe was rich. The thought rattled around in his brain, not gaining purchase. That was something he'd never considered—at all. But if she was rich, why didn't she drive one of those hundred thousand dollar cars so popular in Los Angeles? But if she lived in Europe and not here...

"Why do you drive a bus? You didn't say *that* was your passion," she asked, interrupting his thoughts about what it would mean to date someone with money.

The room filled with the sound of a low hum.

"It's my job. Like you draw those comics," he answered.

The hum came and went again. Reluctantly, Zoe threw the covers from her legs and went to the other room. She came back with a phone.

"But art has always been my passion. If yours is this love of watches—"

"Horology—"

"If your passion is...horology...then why aren't you doing that?"

"Is that about your dad?" he asked, pointing to the phone.

"No, it's missed calls from my brother. Probably wants me to come over and look at their baby again. I don't get babies.... Sorry, you were saying why you don't do whatever a horologist does for a living?"

"I'm happy with my job, if that's what you're asking."

"Really. Hmmm. Okay." Zoe fiddled with the switch on the side of the phone. It rang in her hand, the sound loud and clear this time. She swiped across the glass and answered with a huskily murmured greeting.

"Nicki? What?" Zoe's face morphed from mild annoyance to scared in a heartbeat. "UCLA this time. Right. Fine, I'll be there."

"What's wrong?"

"Papa collapsed again. He's at UCLA." Zoe discarded the robe and rifled through her backpack, pulling out jeans and a long sleeved T.

Realizing he was naked as she was, Max jumped from the bed and untangled his clothes from the bedcovers.

"Do you need a ride?" He'd seen a lot of cars outside but didn't think one was hers.

"Yeah...no...I don't know." She hesitated a long moment, holding white tube socks in one of her hands. The phone was still gripped tightly in the other.

"Can you drop me off...out front?" she said as she slipped into sneakers, gathered and threw stuff haphazardly into the small knapsack he'd seen her carry.

"I'm happy to come in if you need the moral support."

"Max. Thanks. I just need a ride. Not a bunch of questions from my family."

As they drove in silence weaving their way through traffic from Los Feliz to Santa Monica, he wondered if the questions would be about who he was or what he did.

SEVEN

Zoe

Zoe patted the pockets of her jeans. She came up empty. Her keys and phone were missing. Before she let her heartbeat accelerate too fast and panic set in, she looked around the waiting room, trying to remember where in the hell she'd put everything.

"What's wrong?" Nicki asked. Zoe wasn't so self-centered that she didn't see the exhaustion lines creasing her brother's brow. A new fiancé, a baby, and a sick dad couldn't be easy. She didn't want to add grouchy sister to the list.

"I think I must have left my stuff in the car I got a ride in," she answered as if lost personal stuff was as insignificant as a bug bite.

"Crap. Was it one of those share cars?" Nicki hands tunneled through his hair. "They have the phone number in the app, right?"

Nope, not a share car. Max might be in the business of driving others around. But not in his little red Toyota.

"I left my phone too," she said, avoiding the issue of Max. "No number."

Nicki fingered his phone. "I'll download the app, then you can sign in and call."

Resigned to having to discuss her sex life with her brother, Zoe was about to correct her brother's misunderstanding when Max did it for her. The hairs on her arm literally rose in awareness of Max. His musky scent tickled her nostrils.

"Zoe. Sorry I took so long. But I wanted to park first." He handed her the leather backpack that had been so all-fire important a moment ago. "Your phone is in that pocket," he said, gesturing to one of the bulging outer pockets.

Her "thanks" was sheepish. Now that her mind was a bit clearer, she recalled Max *had* said something about parking when she'd jumped from the car like it was on fire. The urge to check on her dad and prevent her two worlds from colliding had been at the front of her mind. But she'd let Nicki's wolf cry do it once again. Her dad was somewhere getting tested and wouldn't be checked into a room for at least an hour. She could have showered off Max's smell and caught a ride share car. Instead, she was stuck trying to avoid awkward moments.

Max didn't stand on ceremony or appear to be easily embarrassed. Without waiting for an introduction, he extended his hand to her brother. "Max. You Nick or Adonis?"

"Nick." Her brother shook her lover's hand with certainty. "Thanks for bringing my sister over."

"Not a problem. We were…having dinner anyway."

Zoe was trying to think of a way to clarify. Not make

it seem like she had been swinging from the chandelier before she'd arrived. But her explanation was cut short by the arrival of her other brother.

Fuck.

She didn't need this now.

At all.

The sudden surge of adrenaline fueled anger at seeing her *other* brother made her tremble. *This* was half the reason she needed out of the U.S. The country wasn't big enough for the two of them.

"Did you take care of what you needed to get Dad off the hook?" Nicki asked Adonis.

"Yeah. The job site's sorted out. I'll head back up to Malibu tomorrow. Hart agreed to me taking over. Showed her my portfolio. I may not have all the old world charm of dear old dad, but she's finally releasing him from his contract."

"Good." Nicki bobbed his head. "One less thing to worry about. Driving up to Malibu every damned day made no sense in his condition."

"How's he doing?" Adonis asked. "Do we know what in the hell is going on?"

The anger vibrating through her body cut off Zoe's power to speak.

"Max," her traitor of a date said as he extended his hand to her tall brother with the model good looks that more than lived up to his name. Maybe if her dad had named her Athena.... Zoe couldn't complete that thought process. Nothing made the past change. It was as fixed as concrete. "You must be Adonis, the other brother," Max continued, shaking her older brother's hand.

"Good to meet you." Adonis took in Max's casual pants and shirt. Zoe's brother's eyebrows knitted together in confusion. "Should I know you?"

It was time for Zoe to step in. Smooth over the introductions. That's what a normal person would have done. But she couldn't. Her relationship with Adonis was anything but normal. Nope, relationship was the wrong word for what was left between her and her brother. They shared blood—bad blood.

"What are you doing here?" Zoe asked, her tongue, lips, and teeth finally able to process the question that had been rattling in her brain for the last few moments.

"He's my dad too," was Adonis' reply.

That answer wasn't enough. It broke a longstanding pact they'd reached more than a decade ago. "I came here on the condition I didn't have to see you." To Nicki she said, "Those were the rules. Those have always been the rules."

"Dad's health trumps that," Adonis said with irritating authority.

"Since when do you give a rat's ass about anyone else? You've certainly moved on in life like nothing ever happened."

"Zoe—"Nicki's voice was a warning shot across the ship's bow.

"Don't 'Zoe' me. We agreed that I wouldn't have to see him. We've never done holidays, Sunday dinners, none of this—for a very good reason, Nicki."

"Dad wanted to see you. I did whatever I needed to get you here."

"So you lied? Is that—"

The authoritative throat clearing that had probably been going on for more than a minute finally penetrated the red haze fogging Zoe's eyes and ears. Lifting her thumb and middle finger to her mouth, she let out the piercing whistle her dad had taught her when she was a kid.

Sweet silence filled the small waiting room.

"Zoe Andreis. Dominic's daughter." She extended her hand to what had to be the nine thousandth lab coat-wearing person she'd seen in the last month.

By Zöe Andreis

"Dr. Gallardo." His self-introduction was unceremonious. The doctor's handshake was cold and weak. Her confidence in the doctor went down a notch. "Your father has a pulmonary embolism."

"What does that mean?" Zoe asked instead of, 'is he going to die?' which is what she really wanted to know.

"He's been administered the anticoagulant Warfarin. We'll continue Heparin while we keep an eye on him.

Luckily, we caught this early. DVT in patients like him have the lowest level of recurrence."

"How low?" Max asked.

"Three percent," Dr. Gallardo answered. "If you'll excuse me," the doctor said, turning and disappearing through double doors festooned with bright red stickers barring normal mortal admittance.

WANDERLUST

By Zöe Andreis

Zoe rounded on Max. "Do you know what in the hell he was talking about?"

Max pulled her two hands into his. The warmth spread through her body, replacing the cold that had seeped into her bones.

"Your dad has some deep vein thrombosis." He must have taken in her clueless look because he took a deep breath and started again. "He has a blood clot. They usually start in the legs. The problem comes when the clot lodges in the lungs or the heart. Your dad's got stuck in his lungs. It's probably what caused the weakness, collapsing, fainting spells and the chest pain—all the stuff that freaked out your brothers and brought you to the States. So it sounds like they've admitted him and given him a blood thinner as the first line of treatment. They're going to follow that up with a second kind of anti-blood thinner. Given this treatment, the doctor thinks the likelihood of this not happening again is ninety-seven percent."

Adonis stopped, staring, mouth opened, and snorted. "Are you dating a doctor? That's way above your usual."

"I'm not dating…He's not…And you all think I'm being an asshole. There's exhibit one. You know what? None of this matters. Sounds like Papa's out of the woods." To Max she said, "You think we'll be able to see him soon?"

"Maybe an hour or so? I'd go ask at the nurses' station."

Zoe gave Nicki a meaningful look. Her youngest brother yoked an elbow around the eldest's neck and led him toward the blue garbed men and women at the other end of the short hall.

"How did you know all that?" she asked, suddenly grateful Max hadn't dropped her in front of the revolving door.

"My mother had some...medical problems..." Max looked everywhere but at her.

"Oh. How did she do?"

"She was on the bad end of the prognosis. They didn't catch her clots until much later. Women don't present the same symptoms as men. She didn't make it out of the hospital."

"Oh!" Zoe's hand came to her mouth involuntarily. "I'm so sorry. I had no idea. You didn't say anything last week."

"Kind of a mood killer," he said quietly.

"But I was talking about my dad..." It would have been natural, she wanted to say but didn't. Death was the natural consequence of life, but didn't make for great first date conversation. Despite the way her brothers acted, like death was around every corner, she got it.

"And he's going to be fine from the looks of it." Max brought her hands together and kissed her fingertips. "Be grateful for that."

"I'm sorry I was such an ass earlier," Zoe acknowledged. "I'm glad that you came."

"What's up with your brother?"

"Speaking of mood killers. Maybe another time on my parents' firstborn, the great and wonderful Adonis. Suffice it to say that there's no bridge that can cover the gap between us. He did something unforgiveable, but walks around a free man." She shook her head at the unfairness of the so-called justice system.

"We can see Dad now," Nicki said as he came back into the waiting room. "He's in six thirty-two. He asked for you, Zoe. But we can only go in one at a time—family only."

Max dropped her hands. Even with the worry about her father, the loss of the comfort her lover's touch brought was oddly acute. "I'll wait outside. Get some air. I can drive you home," Max said.

"I'm not sure how long I'm going to stick around," she said. Zoe closed her eyes for a long moment, and lowered her head in contemplation. Adonis and Dominic were enough to handle. Max was the tipping point on the scale. She needed to avoid overload. "Please go. I'll call you later."

"Sure thing," Max said, starting toward the elevators.

"Dismissed," Adonis said with heavy emphasis on each syllable. "Not keeping him around, are you? Can't remember one that lasted."

"You know what? No one asked you. I don't see any women in your vicinity. But that's not too shocking as you killed the first one."

"Hey! Hey, sis—you go see Dad…Now!" Nicki, the youngest child peacemaker, yelled.

It *had* been below the belt. But if anyone deserved the hit, Adonis did.

EIGHT

Max

Not five seconds after the parking lot arm swung down behind his car, muted buzzing filled Max's car.

Zoe.

He shouldn't have walked away when she'd obviously needed him so much.

He'd been a wuss to leave. But family drama wasn't his thing, for one. He didn't stay where he was unwanted, for another.

The phone vibrated against the seat again. Flouting every traffic law on the books, he picked up the gadget and swiped at the glowing green button.

"Zoe?" he queried as he pressed the plate glass screen to his face.

A throat cleared. Oops. Not Zoe. "I'm trying to reach—"

"This is Max Kiss," he said, clearing his own throat.

"This is the L.A. County Sherriff's department," the voice said. Max swerved to the right, pulling into an empty metered space on Wilshire. The red blinking light alerting him the meter didn't have a minute left—pulsed. Bad omen. "We have your dad down at the station."

With those words, his worst nightmare came to life. He'd been staring down the barrel of this particular shotgun for the last eighteen months. His father had finally pulled the trigger.

"What do you mean?" he asked, desperately clinging to the idea that his assumptions were wrong. There was always the slimmest chance his dad was down at the station for an entirely different reason than the one he'd imagined.

"We found him wandering along Soledad Canyon Road." Nope, not one iota wrong. This wasn't different. Instead, it was the same, but worse.

How quickly his night had changed from the very promising start in line at the sushi place. There it had been all smiles and warm Japanese greetings. Now it was hospitals and police stations. Max glanced at the watch Zoe had admired earlier. "I'll be there in an hour. I'm in Beverly Hills."

"Ask for Sergeant McGinley." The phone went dead.

For long stretches, the traffic was at a near standstill. His mind pinged back and forth between Zoe and the inevitable decisions facing him about his dad. By the time he got on to the 118, Max figured he must have heard wrong in the elevator lobby. Zoe's brother had killed a woman. And he was walking the earth like a free man? He shook his head and moved to what looked like a faster lane. He'd streamed too much Netflix drama. The sheer craziness of popular anti-heroes was going to his head.

The world wasn't full of misanthropes and murderers. At least he hoped not.

The benches lining the wall at the station were empty when Max walked in. Maybe there'd been one big mix-up. Maybe his father was home sleeping the night away while someone else's dad was warming a cot. Shoving his hand into his pocket, he crossed his index and middle finger.

"Max Kiss. Sergeant McGinley?" he questioned while trying to seek out a nametag or badge on the shirt.

The guy Lieutenant Huff, not Sergeant McGinley, jerked his thumb toward the back of the station.

Long seconds later, another officer put down some papers and rose.

"You related to…" he picked up what looked like a driver's license, "Miklós Kiss?"

He'd heard both names mispronounced more times than he could remember. But it wasn't worth correcting anything now, mispronunciation or not, it wasn't a mix-up. His dad was here somewhere.

"He's my father."

"So you're gonna want to get some kind of home health aide, or put this guy in a secure nursing facility. He can't be alone."

"I'll take him home," Max said, ignoring the ad hoc advice. "Where is he?"

"In a holding cell." McGinley jiggled some keys on a chain at his waist. "I'll get him —"

"Why is my father in a cell?" Max demanded. Admittedly Miklós had some issues, but criminality wasn't among them.

McGinley didn't hesitate for a moment. "The safety of my officers is the first priority."

"He's eighty one and not a brawler," Max retorted.

"Tell that to Officer Sanders," he said, pointing toward a small kitchenette.

Max looked through the door. The freezer door slammed. A young man in uniform turned around. In his hand was an ice pack. His left eye was black, blue, and swollen shut.

Shit.

"He hasn't been this violent before," Max offered.

"But he's been violent." Sergeant McGinley wasn't asking a question. His world-weary expression said he already had the answer.

"Nothing I couldn't handle." The doctors had warned him. His father had been a big man, but burly had softened to elderly. Max had muscled through the bad days. No one had gotten a black eye.

"Where does your dad live?" McGinley asked.

"Paraguay Drive."

"That's at least four miles from where we found him."

"He's got long legs." His dad may not be as big, but he was still a tall imposing man who'd grown up walking miles daily. A stretch of the Santa Clarita valley probably hadn't been much of a challenge.

"You doing this alone?" McGinley squinted at him. The man's blue eyes pierced his veneer of denial.

Max considered lying. Inventing a whole passel of siblings who were in town to lend a hand with round the clock care. But there didn't seem to be any sense in mistruth.

"Kinda. Yeah. I check on him around my work schedule."

"Hmm. Come on back." McGinley's hand went under the counter. A buzz and click sounded. He pulled a half door open and beckoned Max to follow.

Through a maze of metal desks empty save stacks of official looking forms, and file boxes piled high, Max weaved before they got to an area in the back. A deputy sheriff stood guard, keys on belt, looking bored.

"He's here for number three," McGinley said to the guard.

Two minutes of jingling and sorting ensued before the deputy put his hand on the right key. The unlocked door swung outward. In the antiseptic cell, his father sat, sans shoes and belt, hunched over mumbling to himself. Nothing in life prepared you for this kind of thing. You were born to a mom whom you thought knew everything, to a dad who was the strongest man in the world. A few decades later, every fantasy you had was shattered by the reality of age and illness.

"Dad? It's me Max," he said, leaning into the small cinderblock room. "I've come to take you home."

"Where in the hell have you been?" Miklós yelled. "They've got me in here like I'm some *bűnös*."

"What did he say?"

"It's just a word for a criminal. I'm sure he doesn't understand why he's in jail if he didn't do anything."

"We're not charging him with socking that deputy."

Max cursed himself at his choice of words. Punching someone wasn't nothing. "Sorry. I'll take him now. Where are his shoes and stuff?"

The key-jingling guard stepped away for a moment and came back with his father's belongings in a giant plastic zip top bag. Max took the bag and extracted the contents. Kneeling, he slipped on his dad's leather shoes, so very out of place in sunny southern California, looped the belt around Miklós' thinning middle, hooking the prong into the last hole, and helped up the man who was nearly as tall as he. Thanking the officers profusely, Max got out of the station as quickly as possible. He didn't want anyone changing their mind about dragging his dad through the criminal justice system. He may hate the idea of nursing homes, but county jail had to be far worse.

Miklós was mercifully silent during the short drive home. Max helped him out of the car, out of his clothes and into bed. Going against his anti-drug rule, he shifted the stale cereals and crock pot from above the fridge and opened the cabinet behind them. There, in an old Tupperware were medications Dad's gerontologist had prescribed. Not wanting Miklós to turn into one of those zombies that lined the corridors of hospitals and nursing homes, he'd taken the prescriptions, had them filled, but had refused to administer the drugs. But thoughts of battling against his father's likely resistance when he woke in a few hours prematurely exhausted Max.

Reading the labels carefully, he chose among the brown bottles and palmed a single tablet. After he filled a plastic tumbler from the tap, he brought both the medicine and water to his father. Though Miklós hadn't resisted getting into bed as he had many nights before, he was anything but resting and asleep. His arms and legs flailed like he was drowning in a pool—not prone on a queen size.

"Here." He offered the pill and water to his father without explanation.

Either tired or unusually compliant, Miklós took and swallowed both. Twenty minutes later the rustling of sheets turned to snores. Max eased Miklós down into what he hoped was a comfortable position then tiptoed from the room.

Three o'clock the watch read. The distant howl of coyotes and the occasional engine motor were the only sounds breaking the nighttime silence. About nine hours and a world away from Zoe and green tea ice cream. He sat on the hideous couch his mother had loved in the department store showroom, but had hated in the house, and let his mind drift toward the beginning of the night. How had this Greek goddess walked into his life and fulfilled fantasies he hadn't even known he had?

Pounding snapped him to wakefulness. Disorientation fogged his brain. He bashed his knee on his way to the front door. Fortunately, his brain cleared enough for him to ask who was knocking before opening the door.

"DPSS."

He fished in the alphabet soup of his brain, but came up empty. "Who?" he asked, cracking open the door security chain width. A short woman opened a leather portfolio and fished out a card. She slipped into his hand.

Kathi McNabb was scribbled across the card in ink. The rest, printed, read: Department of Public Social Services. Adult Protective Services. Civil servants were popping up like popcorn these days.

"How can I help you?" he asked, resisting the strong urge to shut the door against the reality and inevitability creeping in. He didn't need a watch to know that eight in the morning wasn't yet a decent hour for visitors.

"I'm here to do a welfare check. L.A. County Sherriff referred us after an incident last night. Can I come in?"

Faster than he was prepared for, the other heavy black shoe was about to drop to the earth. It had only been a matter of time until this happened. Reluctantly, he pushed the door closed and slid the flaking gold tone chain from its moorings.

"Max Kiss." Formally, he held out his hand.

Flustered, the woman moved the portfolio from one hand to the other and gave him a limp squeeze. He backed away from the door and walked purposefully to the dining room table.

Kathi took the hint and set up shop. First, she took out a manila folder. Several pamphlets and flyers followed.

"What's your father's name?"

Max's sigh was long. "Do we have to do this? He's home safe. He's asleep in the bedroom. I'm here keeping an eye on him."

"What happens when you have to go back to work, school, or your family? We need to make sure your dad is safe."

"Miklós Kiss," he supplied, though he was sure she already knew the answer.

They spent the next five minutes doing the pronunciation and heritage dance as if his father were the first immigrant to wash up on America's shores.

"What's his diagnosis? Miklós Kiss." This time she

turned the 's' into the 'sh' sound it was in Hungarian. Close enough.

"Alzheimer's. Middle stage."

"How often has he wandered off?" Kathi asked, pen poised.

"This is only the second time." He kept his face neutral, trying not to wince. Out loud, it sounded worse than it had been.

"Only! You're aware he could have been hurt? Seriously injured?" she asked, her voice's pitch going higher with every word.

"Of course."

Kathi laid her hand on the shiny tri-fold papers she'd laid down earlier and slid them across the table. "I think you should consider 'round the clock care."

"I'm doing what I can," Max said. "It's under control. Last night was an…an…aberration. I'll be more diligent in coming up." Guilt nearly knocked him from the chair. He'd been more concerned about getting his rocks off than making sure his father was cared for properly. He pushed any thoughts of a repeat performance with Zoe from his mind. He wouldn't make the same mistake twice. Couldn't.

She smiled one of those mommy-like smiles that made him feel like a sixteen-year-old again. "Date?"

"Won't happen again." He made his voice as firm as his conviction had to be.

"That's just it…Max was it? How fast this disease progresses is unknown, but the prognosis isn't. He's going to get worse. Whether that's five months or five years, we don't know. But no one expects you to live like a monk for that long a time."

But that's what he'd been doing. Maybe Zoe wouldn't have gotten so deep under his skin so quick if he hadn't been living like a Catholic priest. But he had to do it. When his mother had gotten sick, he'd been so busy trying to date, pick up extra shifts so he could afford to date, and keep up with the guys from work, that he hadn't kept an eye on her. So it still seemed as if she'd been tired one day and dead the next. If he'd known those were her last days, none of the other would have mattered. It didn't matter now. Not really. But on the day of her funeral, when she was buried at her family's cemetery, he'd promised himself to stay by his father's side if he got ill. Max didn't expect that to be mere months after his mother died. But that promise still remained.

"I've been looking into a home health aide," he offered. He'd started the search. But it had been just one more thing on his ever growing to do list. It wasn't like he'd had a desk job so he'd kicked the can down the road.

"How many hours would you get?"

"I was thinking eight."

"Max, in all honesty, I think you've passed that stage. Can you move up here? Can you commit to having someone fill in the other sixteen hours you aren't here?"

"He'd need that many hours?"

"You would 'cause he's awake most nights, isn't he?"

"His doc gave me pills that could fix his Circadian rhythm." Max didn't mention he hadn't tried them past the first two weeks because zombie Miklós wasn't the kind of quality of life he wanted for his father.

"For now. But what about two weeks from now? Two months from now? Two years?"

"I only have to decide what to do today, maybe tomorrow. I'll take some days off, let everything settle down." He didn't know how in the hell he'd manage that, but he didn't share that detail with Kathi.

"If you believed in only living for now, you'd be a day laborer in an SRO hotel. But you've probably got savings, a pension. You're planning for tomorrow with everything in your life except your father."

Max stood. Stuck out his right arm, a sharp ninety degree angle to his body. "Thanks for stopping by. I've got things covered from here."

"This isn't it, Mr. Kiss. The county can take further measures if you don't get the help you need."

"Great. Thanks." He ushered her out and closed the door behind Kathi with a solid thud.

All the inelegant solutions to his dad's care whirred through his mind as he picked up the newspapers from the last three weeks. He could have sworn he'd bundled them for recycling already. Maybe his dad wasn't the only one losing memory.

"Zsófia! Where are you?"

Max dropped the papers like he had those weeks before. Déjà vu pulled him in as he realized he had done this exact pivot before. He was going to have to tell his father that his mother was dead. For the fifth time—not that he was counting.

NINE

Dominic

Zoe jammed her pinkies into her mouth and whistled as loud as she could. Everyone in Dominic's living room fell silent.

"You're making me regret I taught you that," he said from his perch on the couch. The small crowd assembled in his apartment laughed. "Good thing the folks upstairs aren't home."

He loved his daughter. She was his heart and soul, maybe even his left arm. But he worried that being tall would make it hard for her to find someone. Between that and her manly Chicago whistle, it would take a special guy to appreciate all his daughter's other charms. God, he hated getting old. He'd gone from worrying about his love life to that of his children. God save him if he started praying for more grandkids to dote on.

"I know you all like social media and all that endless fiddling with your phones," Zoe started, interrupting his thoughts on planning her future, "but I like to see people in person. So here's what we're gonna do. I made this weekly calendar." She did her best Vanna White imitation at the large sectioned off white board on the wall. Dominic tried not to wince at the holes she'd probably made in his wall to hang the board. He wondered if he had enough spackle or was a trip to the hardware store going to be necessary. Nick and Adonis knew what to do with a hammer and nail. His Zoe, not so much.

When he'd gotten all three kids miniature tool belts, she'd filled hers with colored pencils and a sharpener. He looked away from the white board and took in his grown daughter. At least she'd settled into her own skin. He remembered that awkward slouching stage where it looked like his five foot ten daughter wanted to disappear —shrink into a petite version of herself. He tuned her back in again. She was still talking calendars and sched- ules. "Starts with Sunday, ends with Saturday. Each day is broken up into four-hour shifts from eight a.m. to eight p.m. We'll try this for two weeks then regroup."

He got that itchy feeling in his bones again. The one that drove him nuts when someone was helping him instead of him helping someone. "This is totally unneces- sary. Baby Iris needs this kind of care, I don't," Dominic grumbled. "You need to make a chart for her."

Not that Holly and Nick and their friends didn't have a handle on that baby's care. But he'd once been a part of that group giving Nick and Holly a break. It was crappy being the *sick* grandparent. The old guy everyone stood around like he was a cancer patient on the verge of death. He looked around the room fully expecting a Catholic priest there, beads in hand, ready for last rites.

"You don't get to decide, Dad," Zoe said. Her tone brooked no argument. He didn't make one. Exhaustion etched her face. Tired of being the main person responsible for him, she'd called in reinforcements. He couldn't blame her. Wouldn't undermine her either. He didn't want her sacrificing her life for his, though he'd gladly do it the other way around.

"You're all treating me like I'm some senile nursing home patient," he said, unable to help the self-pity he heard in his own voice. So much for the promise he'd made to himself not a few minutes ago. But who in the hell wanted to be surrounded by rubbing alcohol and pity?

"Maybe if you stopped acting like you were some senile nursing home patient....Let's see." Zoe flexed her left hand wide open. She started ticking off his numerous violations against her fingers. "You...misplaced your compression stockings, haven't used the foam wedge we got, and Nicki says you've even driven up to Malibu once this week even though you're not supposed to be sitting for long periods of time. I may not have been in So Cal in a while, but nothing says sedentary like the PCH during rush hour."

"I'm *not* an invalid," he whined, then immediately regretted it when Zoe looked poised to add another week of round robin babysitting to the empty space at the bottom of the calendar.

"I'm off Tuesday next week," Sophie Reid interrupted. "I'll do twelve to four. Getting over from the Valley should be fine that time of day. I so owe you one, Dominic."

"You don't have to do this, Sophie," Dominic said. He'd given her a ride a couple of times, fixed some stuff at her place for no charge. But she didn't need to pay him back for that.

"You've helped me out, no questions asked," she said. "Returning the favor is all."

Everyone else picked from the cup of rainbow markers and filled in shifts. How she'd found a different color for each person, he wouldn't ask. It was the crazy kind of thing that mattered to her and no one else.

He watched the action moving around him like a dock in a swift current. Zoe was careful to get everyone's phone number below their name. Times surely had changed. When he was coming up, an appointment was just that. Now everyone wanted a call before you left. A call when you were on your way. A call when you were almost there. Sometimes he wondered what in the hell Angelenos had done before cell phones and texting. All this constant communication seemed like an excuse not to show up.

"We're missing Friday afternoon," Zoe announced while tapping at the board with the hard end of a bright red marker. "I can't do it. I have a conference call with the syndicate." Pointedly, Zoe looked around the room. "Anyone. Bueller. Bueller." Not a smile from anyone. Damn somber group. He and his Zoe had watched that movie a dozen times while she'd suffered through adolescent chicken pox. "It's not a funeral, people. And that *was* funny."

If he hadn't been feeling so damned sorry for himself Dominic would have laughed.

A vaguely familiar woman about his age raised her hand. "I'll do it." Now who in the hell was she? The woman's blue eyes looked at him as if they saw right through his bullshit. He hadn't been appraised so frankly in a good long time. Maybe he didn't want to know who she was.

"Sorry, I don't remember your name," Zoe said to the woman. Good manners he'd raised his daughter with.

"Bridget. I'm Ryan's mom," she said, pointing to the sandy haired guy with Sophie. Ah, that was where the resemblance was.

"Okay. Thanks. We're good then." His daughter picked up first one packet, then another from the stack of multicolored paper. He loved that his daughter was a rainbow in a sometimes black and white world. "Here are the care instructions," she started, making sure everyone had a copy in their hands. "They're pretty simple. But my number's on the bottom if you have any questions. And on the parking. Street cleaning is on Monday and Tuesday from noon until three. The city tickets are expensive I hear, so you might want to read the signs when you're parking. That's all."

Now this was what being couch bound did. His eyes zeroed in on the trim figure and sparkly shoes of the only woman he didn't know too well. There, across the room, was Bridget, a nice lady he'd like to chat up. Did he take the blanket off his legs and show off his lady tights as he slip slided toward her? Or did he beckon her over so she could be enveloped in the smell of menthol rub. Ben-Gay wasn't Old Spice.

Choices. Choices.

Damned blood clot.

Patience, he admonished himself as he watched Zoe make her way over to the woman with the piercing blue eyes. Extending her hand, he watched his daughter formally introduce herself. "Bridget?" He strained his ears to pick up more of the short conversation.

"Yep," Bridget answered. Guessed she wasn't the wordy sort.

"Do you know my dad?"

"Nope. But our kids know each other."

"Let me introduce you." Beckoning Bridget to follow, Zoe pushed her way through the lingering folks toward him. He tried to sit up a little taller so that he didn't look like a sultan waiting for grape bearers.

"Dad? This is Bridget. Sorry, didn't get your last name."

"Becker." She extended her hand to Dominic. "You're the sick guy."

"That I am. Looks like my nurse fantasies are about to come true," he said, unable to stop the reflex to wink before his daughter caught him flirting.

"You kid," Bridget said, but blushed all the same. "I'll keep you on the straight and narrow; no problem. I raised two boys."

"I have two boys myself," Dominic said. "Have a seat. Put your feet up. It's all the rage among the gray haired set."

"Speak for yourself," Bridget said. But she joined him on the sofa. Glad he'd sprung for the wide ottoman, he watched as her jeweled flats hesitantly joined his boots on the studded leather.

"You normally have your feet up on the furniture? Feet on floor had to be one of the first lessons I taught my boys."

Heat climbed Dominic's neck. "No. My boys and girl, too."

"So what's the story?" she pushed.

"I may let my daughter arrange for around-the-clock babysitting. But I draw the line at everyone seeing my lady tights."

"Lady tights?"

Dominic pulled up his jeans about two inches above the suede boot's cuff. The damn tights stretched over his hair stared back at him and Bridget.

"You do look like an old lady. Should I get you some white crepe soled shoes?" Her delivery was as dry as Bob Newhart's. He was thinking dry wasn't bad in a woman's...humor.

"You're funny." She was.

"Maybe some of those black crisscross slippers they sell for a couple of bucks at street markets." Was she flirting?

"God save me." He flirted back.

"We could get a walker for you as well. Because these stupid stockings don't make you look old. But a Zimmer frame definitely puts on the years." She was flirting. He was floored. He thought he'd become invisible to ninety-nine percent of women on the planet. Apparently not. He peeled himself from the soft cushions, sat up a little straighter.

"Thanks." Suave. He was so flabbergasted over the day's turn of events, a simple thank you was all he could muster.

"A dashing guy like you will be fine. I don't imagine it's too tough fighting off the ladies."

"No fighting," he said, throwing his hands in the air. Suave was out the window. Had taken a hike to the desert. "I take all offers."

"Do you, now?" Bridget patted his knee. Rather than take her hand back to her lap, it lingered on his thigh. "I'll have to keep that in mind." The hand that had crept up, patted his thigh. "Rest up for my shift. I take no prisoners."

As quickly as she had appeared, Bridget was gone. The flesh tingled on his knee and thigh, lingering for a long, long minute. Hugs and kisses from children and grandchildren were great, but he missed the companionship of someone his age.

TEN

Zoe

"Where are we going?" Dominic said as he reluctantly tightened the new shoes she'd brought over.

"On a walk." Zoe brandished a white folder. Pastel, bold, and neon sheets peeked out. She'd been careful not to repeat a color. "On page twenty-nine of the instructions from the doctor, it says that you should take a healthy walk every day."

"I got the mail already," her dad huffed. "Picked up some poop left on the tree lawn."

"Seriously? You don't have a dog." Zoe scrunched her nose at the thought of picking up feces. Angelenos were so damned inconsiderate. Not for the first time she wondered why in the hell anyone lived in this city. Europeans lived cheek to jowl yet managed to be nicer than people separated by lawns and fences.

"A lot of neighbors do. I didn't want anyone to find a surprise on their shoe," he said while zipping up his windbreaker.

"Seems like someone else's job, if you ask me. Maybe I'll get you one of those little lawn signs about curbing your dog." She mentally added it to the list of things she'd do for her dad before going back home to Budapest.

"Ah, Zoe. It's no big deal." Her father gestured again to the shoes. "Why white?" he asked. At least they were fastened.

Progress.

"They had these in your size." With no car, one mall was all she could manage.

Her dad looked down at her tightly laced Doc Martens. "I don't see you in cushy sneakers, with Velcro nonetheless. It's no different than the shoes Iris wears."

"I have the keys. Let's go," she said, done with his complaints. If the hospital discharge instructions said walk, then it was time to walk.

Dominic gripped her arm tightly as they made the short journey down the sloping driveway.

"Don't need to add a broken hip and walker to the lady tights and walking shoes," her father joked. Despite his attempt at lighthearted, the anxiety came through in his voice. How had her always strong, in command father been reduced to complaining, annoying patient, and a little bit helpless nonetheless?

Damned if she'd seen it coming. But now, next to him, it was if he'd aged ten years in a few weeks. The top of his head was barely covered with hair that was no longer as dark or as thick as she remembered. He was still fit, but his V frame had morphed into middle-aged granddad bod.

If she met him on the street now, she wouldn't spare him a second glance. He'd be one of those nebulous older gentlemen who walked to diners, held doors open, and complained about aches and pains. Not the father who'd built her a platform bed or singlehandedly converted her walk-in closet into a teenager's dream bathroom so she didn't have to share with her brothers.

They walked along the street in companionable silence until they reached Beverly Boulevard. "Right or left?"

"Left. Since you were last here, there are a thousand new stores on Beverly. Can't figure out how they make money only selling cookies, or ice cream or appetizers. Every store has a one word name. What do these people offer in Crave? What do they sell in Stir? Milk? Please."

"Have you thought of moving to Greece?" Zoe asked. If she couldn't be closer to her father, maybe she could bring her father closer to her. Somewhere she could keep an eye on him. He'd been so content in Los Angeles that she'd never dared bring it up. But it was important for all of them to plan for his future.

"In this political climate? I hear there are lines in the banks, riots in the streets. Sounds like the Depression."

"I don't think mighty Grecian empire is going to collapse like the Romans, Papa." Zoe rolled her head from side to side. The news was so damned negative. Every place except the U.S. was on the verge of extinction if you believed American newspapers. She knew better than to start a discussion about propaganda, though. "You could sell this duplex. Get a really nice place outside the city. Grow olives, or grapes or something."

"What about Iris?"

That name. She sort of understood how her brother had let his wife name their baby after their long deceased mother. But it still socked her in the heart every single time she heard it uttered. Her dad was peering at her. Right. Greece.

"Last time I checked," she continued, "there were airports and runways in Athens. I'd be happy to move with you." Though after she'd said it, Zoe had no idea how she'd make that work. She'd already 'done' Greece. Her fan mail told her that readers were looking for her to go in a new direction.

"What about my business?" her dad asked.

"Aren't you ready to retire? If not, I'm sure there are more than enough renovations on all those old houses over there to keep you busy for years. You always talk about old world construction. You could experience it firsthand."

"My Greek is rusty," was the next excuse from him. They'd been pretty weak so far. Given enough time, she was starting to think she could wear him down.

"But it's not non-existent. Yaya and Pappoús spoke only Greek at home. You'll brush up in a week or two. Think about it. I'd love it if you were close by. It's not the same with you six thousand miles away."

"You live in Budapest, not Athens."

"So, come stay with me there. I'm in Hungary for maybe another six months, tops. Krakow is next. I hear it's beautiful. You could have coffee in the morning. Maybe go to museums in the afternoon. Live in a different European city every few years. It's an amazing opportuni-ty." She knew firsthand. She'd lived it. Grateful every day that her job allowed her to live her dream.

"I'd be bored out of my gourd in two weeks. Have you ever known me to sit around sipping tea with my pinky in the air?" Her dad mimed his Queen Elizabeth tea-drinking style. "Maybe you think I'm like that now because of these stupid tights." He stopped to lift the cuff of his jeans for the five hundredth time.

"Enough with the compression stockings, Papa. They were prescribed and you have to do it. I was just thinking out loud." Zoe paused while a Bentley turned the corner at an unsafe speed. If they'd had a toe in the street, it would have been run over. "I worry about you. I want you to live a long time. Is that so bad?"

"I love you too, Zoe bear." They walked along another tree-lined block before Dominic spoke again. "My birthday is coming up."

"What would you like? I can get you some great European walking shoes. After I got your sneakers, I saw that there were some stores in Beverly Hills or the Valley that specialize. We could go early, beat the crowds. Maybe have lunch."

"So, that would be a nice gift...or...you could move back here," Dominic said softly. She could barely hear his voice over the nonstop traffic rushing along the boulevard. Was there ever a moment of peace in this city? Did the cars ever stop?

"Back? I never lived here to begin with." Adonis had moved first. She'd gone to Pratt. Then her father had sold her childhood home, taken Nick, and moved west to join his brother like he'd planned decades earlier.

"You know what I mean. Nick and Holly and little Iris are out here."

Her mom's name. Again. That alone was enough to keep her from the City of Angels. It would take years to get used to 'Iris, this,' and 'Iris, that' not sparking that little bit of grief in her heart.

"Nick went to high school in California after you moved. It's only natural that he live here, I guess. Plus he's in the entertainment business," she conceded. But that didn't mean either one of them had to be in this place that considered a car show, culture.

"Don't you want to get to know your little niece?"

"I'm here now. I was here for a weekend after she was born. We'll get to know each other over time. There are a lot of years between now and her eighteenth birthday."

"Children benefit from the love of as many people as are able," he said in the old man with wisdom voice that she'd rarely heard from her dad before this visit. Nothing like a brush with death to turn up the schmaltz.

"Umm, okay Papa. Got you. I'll try to visit more often," she started. "But you know I have a job that kind of requires that I travel."

"Wanderlust?"

"The very same. The title isn't exactly Canoga Park or something that suggests a certain place."

"I liked that one you did about pastry," her dad acknowledged, looking out of the corner of his eye. He'd always said he read it, but they didn't talk much about her work. The one thing that took her away from the family was a sore topic.

By Zöe Andreis

"No Ziploc bags. Few American foods. No pre-made crusts. It's about adapting to another way of life. It's kind of fun." Zoe made an effort to highlight the positives about her world. No parent wanted to hear about the hard parts. The isolation that came from short shallow relationships with transient women and men who wanted to date you, then marry the girl next door.

"Are you lonely?" he asked, zeroing in on the one question she'd refused to ask herself once in the last decade. That was the hard part.

"I meet new people all the time. I have tons of friends from everywhere in the world," she bluffed. "I travel a lot of weekends to Italy, to Spain, to Switzerland. There's a vibrant expat community abroad. Kind of like the Greek community in Chicago that helped us. Especially after mom died." She looked at the pavement under her feet. Europeans, she'd found, were extremely family oriented. Everything from business to shops were closed much of August. Most expats became families with children. Away they went to the salt caves of Slovakia, the beaches of Montenegro, or the endless villas and cabins in mountains and villages of every country. She'd always maintained the quiet times were good for writing, inking, and painting. But more than once she'd kind of envied others their getaways.

"I've been missing Iris a lot lately, you know," her dad said, interrupting her thoughts. That single sentence nearly halted Zoe in her tracks. If she didn't think about her mother's death, day-to-day life was easier. It was a fundamental wound that she piled a lot of travel, work, and sex on top of. To think of her mother, to think of losing her at that critical time in her adolescence nearly took her breath away.

"Me too, Papa," she managed after swallowing hard at the lump the mere mention of her mother's name formed in her throat.

"I may not have had your mother till the day I die, but I do have someone. I want you to find that special person for you, like Nick has found his Holly." Zoe made a huge effort not to roll her eyes — hard. What was it with the senior set and the urge to set you up? So many women she knew were alone at her age, or in their forties and beyond.

They traveled, saw plays, ate out, and enjoyed a life not tethered to a man's career, his family, his needs.

"I've got time. I need to get more established. Maybe get more traction in some of the smaller and alternative newspapers." All of it was true. She missed regular sex that came with a serious live-in relationship, but the rest, the cooking, the cleaning, the compromise, definitely not any of that.

"What about the guy who came to the hospital?"

"Max?" Zoe coughed to cover up the gasp. To obscure the butterflies in her stomach, she quickened her pace. "No lollygagging, Papa. How do you know about him? You were in a recovery room, by yourself." Flipping through her mental file, she was sure she hadn't mentioned the bus driver on social media. She'd been careful not to veer too sharply from her regular postings of exotic locations and wacky escapades. Her readers wanted adventure, not the slog of real life. Her job was quickie escapes.

"Nicki may have mentioned a guy in the waiting room." Even though her eyes were straight forward, she didn't miss the sly glance in her direction. He was doing his best 'not interested' voice. He lacked the subtlety necessary, though.

"He's a guy I met a few weeks ago." Her shrug was as offhanded as his voice had tried to be.

"And…" Dominic pressed. His once brisk pace slowed to a near crawl.

"Pick up the pace. Healthy walk, not stroll." They took the next half block in record time. Zoe continued, "And what, Dad? We went on a couple of dates. But it's not going anywhere."

"Why not?" Dominic actually looked aggrieved.

"Papa, I love you. You're my favorite parent," Zoe started.

"I'm your only living parent. But what's that got to do with anything?"

"I do not want to discuss my sex life with you."

"Whoa ho. I didn't say anything about sex." Her dad had the same deer in the headlights look he'd had when she'd asked for a ride to Planned Parenthood in high school. "As long as you're being careful …."

"Sex smex, Papa. Dating. Hooking up. Whatever. He was a nice guy. We had dinner. That's all." That wasn't all. But parents and sex didn't belong in the same sentence. As far as she was concerned her parents had only done it three times and her dad had been a monk ever since.

"Why is that all? Did he have bad breath?" Dominic asked, moving from the awkward topic himself.

"No, Papa." He'd tasted really good.

"B.O?"

"He smelled fine." More than fine. She shook her head, trying to mentally bat away that particular sense memory.

"Dirty car?" Dominic asked half-jokingly.

She shook her head. "From what I remember it was clean. His house was clean. His clothes were clean. He could have starred in a commercial for all purpose cleaner."

"So what's wrong with him?" her dad asked as if compatibility and cleanliness were the only factors in a modern relationship. From what she'd seen those were the least of the problems. Career and geographic incompatibility were much bigger issues. She'd had far too many coffees with too many significant others unhappily dragged to a foreign country to underestimate that.

"Nothing's wrong. I'm sure he'd make a great husband for some nurse, or teacher."

"Because?"

"He drives a city bus. He's a nine-to-fiver. He'd probably be most comfortable with another civil service worker. Someone stable. They can come home after work and make roast beef together."

"I'm thinking I must have gone wrong somewhere." Dominic stopped dead in his tracks a couple of miles from where they'd started but five steps from his front lawn.

"What do you mean?"

"Clearly I didn't raise you right." Her dad's tone was less than civil. Shame crept up her neck, though she wasn't yet sure what she'd done to deserve his censure.

"You raised me just fine, Dad. I floss my teeth and pay my bills on time."

"Sounds like you don't respect hard work."

"How can you say that? I respect what you do. It paid for my food, clothes, and college."

"Then why do you think you can't date a bus driver?"

"It's not that, Papa. It's a fine job. He provides transportation for those who don't have any other way of getting about. In a city like L.A., it's practically honorable. Maybe he should be sainted." Some unintended sarcasm snuck through.

"But not good enough for you?" he asked, his Chicago accent growing thicker.

"He lives in Hollywood. I live in Europe. A couple of great dates doesn't change that. I'm here temporarily. I'm sure he understood that going in."

"They're *great* dates now. Hmmmm." Her dad pinned her to the sidewalk with his eyes. "You *could* live here."

"You keep saying that. But it doesn't work for two very solid reasons."

"Number one…"

"Um, my career is based on me traveling."

"You could write another comic strip."

"Are you serious? You know how long it took for me to be accepted by a syndicate and get into as many papers as I am in now?" He had to know her kind of success wasn't easily replicated. He'd watched her send packet after packet, seeing which concepts would fly. Wanderlust had been her ninth try.

"I thought you said the syndicate was too commercial. That they wanted to put cartoon Zoe on mugs, and T-shirts, and mouse pads."

"No one uses mouse pads anymore," she deflected. The work part of work was hard enough without focusing on the crap she liked the least about it.

"You know what I'm saying."

"I may be upset with how they do business. But it's still my job. It pays my bills. For the most part, it makes me happy. I get to draw every day." That had been her seemingly unobtainable childhood dream—achieved.

"What's number two?"

Zoe was quiet for a long moment. She sat heavily on

the front step that bisected the grass. He was pushing too hard. It was time to push back.

"Adonis. Okay. It's Adonis. I know that's not what you want to hear. But California isn't big enough for the both of us."

"You need to forgive your brother."

"Have *you* forgiven him, Papa?"

"He made a mistake," he answered, dodging the question.

"A mistake? That's the worst understatement ever. Maybe those tights are keeping blood from your brain Papa, because he didn't make a mistake. He killed my best friend."

ELEVEN

Max

There wasn't a day he didn't receive mail from one company or another urging him to go digital. "We're becoming a paperless society," everyone said.

By Zöe Andreis

Nevertheless, Max fingered the piece of notebook paper. It had grown soft and pliable in his fingers. The blue ink of her four-two-four number had bled through the fibers.

"How was your week?" Max managed to get out the opening he'd practiced without a slip or stutter.

The sound of pencil scratching on paper nearly drowned out her voice. "Hello! Is this Max the bus driver? How's the big orange bus treating you?" she asked.

Why did people always ask him about the buses like they were his dogs or something? Changing the subject, he asked, "How's your dad?"

Her long sigh was full of about a thousand emotions.

Parents.

Dads, especially.

He got it.

"He's mighty fine," she finally replied. "We're getting him out for long walks. No dizziness. Not lightheaded. A pain in my ass. So it's all good."

Max's laugh relieved much of the tension that had bunched around his shoulders while he continued to finger the soft lined paper. *Get to it already.*

"You busy Sunday morning?" he asked.

"Let's see...I know about ten people in L.A. All of them are busy...so...no. What do you have in mind?" she asked. The scratching of pen on paper had stopped. Her whisky soaked voice was full of humor.

Damn, he'd lost five years and gained fifty gray hairs in her, 'let's see.' He answered, "There's a flea market some Sundays in Pasadena."

"Is that where you get the old watches?" she asked. What sounded like wheels from her drawing chair squeaked. Something hard hit an even harder surface. Sounded like he had her full attention now.

"Yeah, there are sometimes watches, but I like to look for what I can harvest for parts." Realizing how boring that could sound, he backtracked. "I don't have my eye out for anything in particular this month, but I like to have a look around."

"That sounds cool," she said, not sounding turned off about hours of wandering among stalls. He'd made the mistake once of taking a date to an antique market. If the sun hadn't done his date in, the spike heels had been the last blow.

"What time?" he asked, not letting Zoe off the hook. "Early?"

"About ten or so? I can do that. Let me write a note to myself," she said. Scratching started again.

Not knowing if she had an eraser, Max interjected. "No, that's way too late. The latest I've gotten there is five thirty."

"In the morning?" Her laugh was warm and full-throated. Max tried not to think about kissing that spot where her hair curled around her ear. To feel the vibration of that laugh against his lips. "That's practically the night before," came from Zoe in an incredulously loud whisper.

"Eight?" he offered in compromise.

"Nine, if I'm invited the night before," Zoe started, all trace of humor gone. "I'll need sufficient motivation to get me up in the morning."

He thought she'd never ask. "That can be arranged," he said. "What would you like for dinner?"

"Since you're driving, I've got it covered."

♥

Zoe

"I thought of something we could do today," Zoe said as she watched her dad painstakingly put on his walking shoes. He was as bad as a puppy avoiding its new leash.

"Instead of our walk?" Dominic asked, his face and voice full of hope that she'd relent.

"*After* our walk," Zoe replied. She'd taken on the job of taskmaster. She was surprisingly good at it. "The syndicate sent out some e-mail. Studies show sitting is the new smoking." She bent and laced her red Doc Martens to the top.

From: Comic Strip Syndicate
Re: Work related injuries

Warning: Studies show that
long periods of sitting can
lead to...

IF SITTING IS THE NEW SMOKING,
WE'RE ALL GOING TO DIE OF ASS CANCER

Zöe

"Fine," he huffed, standing and advancing toward the door she was holding open. "You want me to sharpen up a pencil and help you draw?"

She led the way down the front walk toward the sidewalk. She turned right instead of left as if that would make a difference. Magnolia, palm, eucalyptus, or ficus. All the unnatural desert greenery was starting to look the same to her.

"It's a comic Papa, not architectural plans," she said, turning back to her father.

"Your brother—"

"I want to make dinner for Max," she said, cutting off whatever he was going to say.

"Dinner? Sounds serious."

Ignoring the high-pitched hope in her father's voice, she laid out her requests. "I was hoping you could help me with sardines, maybe octopus or calamari. Those lemon potatoes you do would be a great side dish."

"Gonna need a lot of lemons."

"Great," Zoe said, orienting herself. She made an about face. "We can walk to the grocery store. Walking with purpose reminds me more of Europe. This random power walking is so L.A."

"The citrus is the easy part," Dominic said, suddenly picking up the pace. "We gotta go to Santa Monica Seafood for the rest."

"Let's get the lemons now, and the rest later," she said. One of the big supermarket chains was only a few blocks away down the busy La Brea thoroughfare. Extra steps would be good for her dad.

"Maybe you should get some of these?" Dominic gestured to his shoes for the thousandth time. If he couldn't wear those damned work boots, he acted like it was the end of the world.

"I could get you a pair of boots like these next time I'm in London," she offered. She couldn't quite see him climbing the stairs of the boot shop weaving between the yellow stitched high top black boots. Best she do that kind of favor for him.

"No need to fly ten hours. I only want shoes without the old people Velcro. They gotta have something like that in the mall."

"Your new granddaughter has Velcro." Zoe had to turn away to hide her smile. It was kind of funny, but

Dominic surely wouldn't think so. Not in his current mood, anyway.

By Zöe Andreis

"Great, babies and me."

Oh…kay, the granddaughter distraction hadn't worked. She'd have to put more in the arsenal, because she was all out of subjects that didn't touch on sensitive topics.

Not all out.

Food was decidedly neutral. She held her father's arm as they crossed the store parking lot. The automatic doors opened with a whoosh. Was evolution going to leave Angelenos with wheels instead of legs?

CANOGA PARK

By Zöe Andreis

"What do you think I should do for dessert?" Zoe asked, doing her Vanna White wave over the store's bakery section.

"You must really like this guy. He gets fresh fish *and* dessert," Dominic said while leading her away from the bakery and over to produce.

"He's brought dinner the last couple of times. My turn to reciprocate, is all."

"How you gonna get the seafood?" her dad baited while he squeezed and bagged lemons.

"Why not here?" she asked, not rising to the implied challenge.

"This part of the Pacific Ocean is polluted. Supermarkets are not for seafood." Her dad strode over to the dairy section. "Damn. A little more notice and we could have done this at the Farmer's Market."

"Are you willing to walk that far? We could do it now."

"These free range eggs look fine. I'm sure there's organic milk somewhere in here."

"I'll call Nicki. He can drive me to wherever you get fish."

"He's upstate shooting for a couple of days. Here's organic cream. That should work."

"What's dessert?"

"*Galaktoboureko.* I haven't met anyone who doesn't like it."

"Phyllo on the top and bottom?"

"Just the way you like it." Dominic paid for the fruit, vegetables, and dairy. Zoe grabbed the bags before Dominic could do the chivalrous thing that was ingrained in his DNA.

"Wanna take the bus?" Zoe pointed her free hand at an Orange bus numbered 212 roaring by.

"You want me to sit for five hours. Plus ride around with seafood. I'll get a new clot *and* stink to high heaven." Dominic's deliberate stare lacked subtlety.

"So what's your brilliant idea? You're dying to share. Go ahead."

They paused at the corner of the street. Zoe jabbed at the tiny yellow button a few times. "Your brother is in town doing a consultation for me. I could ask him to do you a favor. I figure he owes you."

"Maybe we'll run into Max," Zoe said, suddenly warming to the idea of a long quiet bus ride across town. Confrontation was something best avoided.

Dominic's look silenced that train of thought.

"So I'll drive," she said. It had been a long time, but it was like riding a bike, you didn't forget.

"You don't have a license," her father said, quick to point out the illegality of the situation. He'd always been a straight shooter. His little office in the garage was full of notebooks festooned with state licenses, city permits, and required insurance declarations. She had a more creative approach to rules. She'd had a license from the time she was sixteen until twenty-one, that should count for something.

"That's a technicality. It's like riding a bike, I'm sure. Maybe it's time. You being out of commission and all."

"I'm anything but out of commission. I'll drive. You promise not to bitch. Even exchange."

"How long —"

"The longer we talk, the longer it will take." Dominic sped up the pace. Zoe momentarily regretted grabbing for the plastic bags. Handles cut into her palm with every stride. Walking in L.A. was overrated. A quick glance at her father reminded her not to say that out loud.

"The roads are mostly clear now," her father said, interrupting her thoughts about whether she'd be able to hold a pen later. "When do you need this dinner anyway?"

"Tonight."

"Guess you're not babysitting me," Dominic said, stepping up to the door and inserting his key into the lock.

"I switched off with Bridget," she said.

"Maybe we'll double that order."

"What does that mean?" Zoe asked after she put their purchases on his kitchen counter.

"The woman's coming all the way over here. Maybe she'd like some food, not just the smell of what she's missed. This cream's gotta go in the fridge. I know you don't cook much, but you've gotta know that."

"So you're not, like, interested in her or anything?" Zoe asked under her breath, half hoping her father didn't hear or chose not to respond. "The fridges in Europe are really small. You'd really like the fresh from the farm food," she said loud and clear.

"What are you, twelve? With the eye rolling, and not speaking to your brother, I'm thinking you've regressed to your teen years. Want some ripped jeans and black concert T-shirts to go with that sulk?"

CANOGA PARK

By Zöe Andreis

"I don't want anyone to take advantage of you," Zoe said as she stepped up into the passenger seat of her father's pickup.

"I'd like someone to take advantage of me."

"Ewwww. Papa."

"What? I think the proper mourning period for Iris has passed. I'm not aiming for priesthood here."

"Have you checked up on Bridget? Sometimes I read the news wrapped around the funny pages. Older women can take advantage of the few available men."

"I'm not the FBI. I don't do background checks on the *older* women I'm interested in dating."

"So you're thinking about seeing her?" Zoe wanted to feel happy for her dad. He was happy for her. But she had no ability to envision her dad with anyone else besides her mom. To her knowledge, he'd never dated anyone after their mother died.

"Not a secret, Zoe. I think that's what I just said."

"No, you said something about extra portions of food. Geez what's going on here?" Zoe said peering out from the passenger seat of her father's truck. She hadn't been below Third since Nicki had picked her up from the airport.

"What do you mean?"

"All these motels on this street. What is this? We're still on La Brea?"

"They're probably SROs for the nearly homeless. I don't think they're highly ranked on those social media sites everyone talks about."

"Is that a line to get *on* the freeway?" she asked. L.A. was so many contradictions all at once, mansions and shacks, wide boulevards clogged with traffic. It was like city planners didn't exist on this coast.

"The meter's probably on."

"How are you feeling? Should we pull over? Take a walk?"

"It's twenty, maybe thirty minutes tops, dear heart."

"I wonder if driving in L.A. traffic ranks up there with long haul trucking and flying?" Zoe asked, listing two things Dominic had been ordered to avoid. Then, in an instant, the traffic clog eased as if by magic.

"Hardly. Look, the road's clear. We'll be at the edge of the continent in no time.

"Can we take a walk on the beach? I haven't seen the ocean since I've been here. It's what I miss most about being in Greece. Budapest is nice, but landlocked."

"In those boots?"

"They'll survive on the strand."

♥

"DO you need help to the front door?" her father asked her five hours later as he threw the truck into park in front of Max's house. Sand poured from her boots. Strand and Doc Martens didn't mix, it turned out.

No! Zoe yelled in her head. It was enough that her dad was driving to her...to a date. But being handed off was too much like going down the aisle or something. With a sure grip, she hefted the six sealed containers, making sure not to show one hint of weakness. She'd made it one step, then two. The whole thing started to teeter. Her dad stepped out of his truck at the same exact moment Max walked out the front door.

And with that, her two worlds collided.

"Let me help you," Max said, taking the two most precarious containers while her dad pulled an old paper grocery bag from the tiny backseat.

"Do you need this bag? I told you it would be better. But you had to do it your own way."

"Max, this is my father Dominic Andreis. Papa, this is Max Kiss."

"I'd shake your hand, sir, but it's full," Max said, all

polite like a sixteen–year-old on his first date. It was charming and annoying in equal measure.

"Let's get this in the kitchen, then," Dominic said, leading them up the short path to the front door. Inside, her dad glanced around the bungalow, spotted the narrow galley kitchen, and seemed to decide the counter by the stove would have to do. "Where do you eat? There's no table in here."

"There," Max said, gesturing toward a wood table in the corner of the living room. "Or outside."

Or in bed, Zoe thought, remembering their last meal.

"Hmph. Okay."

"Let me show you the house, Mr. Andreis," Max offered.

Max and her dad walked back through to the living/dining area. She tuned out their voices and pulled plates down from the cabinet and cutlery from the drawer, chafing a bit at the familiarity of it. A door opened then closed, and their voices faded. Zoe found glasses and filled one with water from the tap and drank it down. Did it again, but the constriction in her throat still wouldn't ease.

Her friend Amelia had forwarded her an e-mail this morning with an announcement. A new airline was offering two hundred dollar discount flights from California to Europe, with a stopover in Reykjavik. An extra stop in Philadelphia and the priced dropped to a hundred. Maybe she could get her dad out of here for a week. Two stops was usually torture for an impatient traveler like her, but was the right prescription for DVT.

Picturing herself buckling in, flying through the clouds, her throat eased. Adding her father to her mental picture, appropriately suited up in compression tights, made swallowing easier. When her dad and Max came back into the kitchen, she poured the rest of the water into the sink and set the empty class on the counter.

"You sure you don't want me to have a quick look? My tools are right in the truck."

Max shook his head. "I have a kit in the closet. I'll change it out after the flea market this weekend. Maybe I can enlist Zoe to help."

Dominic's head shake was forceful. "I hate to burst your bubble, but hammers and screwdrivers were never her thing."

"Papa. I'm not that bad. I may not be able to build a house from scratch, but even I can fix a leaky sink."

"It's the toilet, dear heart. Constant running is a huge waste of water. Best to fix them quick."

"Do you want to join us for dinner?" Max asked her dad. "From the looks of it, there's more than enough." Zoe's throat eased a little bit more. The clutch in her chest gave way.

"I don't do third wheel," Dominic said. Her dad pulled together the sides of his leather windbreaker and zipped up. "Got a hot date myself. Don't want her food to get cold. Zoe, can you come outside a minute? I need to ask you something."

As quick as it had eased, the anxiety returned. She pulled open the door for her dad, imagining a future where he needed help with all things big and small.

"You need help up?"

"God no, my dear heart. Wanted to tell you that I like

your Max." Her dad said this as if he was giving permission to marry.

"He isn't *my* Max," Zoe said, making sure to emphasize the temporary nature of their relationship. Her father's face had happily ever after written all over it.

"You cooked for him," her father said in the same way someone would say you *married* him.

"If every guy I cooked for was my guy, I'd have a collection."

"Of two, right? I remember you making a pancake breakfast for your high school boyfriend the night after the prom."

"Fine. Two." Zoe hated that about family. They could totally call you on your bullshit. "I like pancakes and seafood and custard. Is this what you wanted to talk to me about? My collection of home cooked meals?"

"No. That wasn't it," Dominic said, propping his foot on the running board. "Are you protected?"

"From what? Leaking toilets?"

"Babies," her father said before a very long sigh. "Don't get me wrong. I like babies. Want more grandkids. But I know the timing isn't right for you."

Zoe wanted to blame the heat creeping up her neck on the sun beating down on them. But it was embarrassment, plain and simple. Never was she so happy that she'd gotten the genes for a dark olive skin tone. Tan skin hid a multitude of sins.

"Got it covered, Dad," she retorted. "I've gotten this far without any babies or a fatal disease. Now why don't you get going? I don't want you to miss your next dose. Remember to take it with food." Zoe slammed the door forcefully. With practiced ease, her father backed the hulking truck out of the space and eased onto the street. Americans sure liked their cars big. Would the roads in Greece fit something like that? Maybe Budapest was a better answer. Maybe her landlord had a two bedroom available and she could transfer her lease.

"Sorry about my dad," she said, turning to the man's heat warming her back, and causing her insides to tingle.

"Don't ever apologize. He's a nice guy. Loves you."

Zoe turned back to the door, making a long show of examining the locking mechanism. She didn't want Max to see the tears she was blinking back. "Hope you like seafood," she said to the dead bolt. "Dad went a little bit overboard."

TWELVE

Dominic

Dominic looked at his watch, then at the clock on the dash, then his watch again. Either he'd completely misunderstood the schedule, or Bridget was very early and entranced by his sage plants. He couldn't say that he was displeased. He'd have liked some time, though, to move newspapers off the couch, maybe vacuum the living room, and wipe down the mess he and Zoe had made in the kitchen. A few minutes to be alone would have been nice too. He could have maybe looked up a couple of things on the computer—like how to date after fifty.

He hadn't lived with anyone in years and had gotten used to doing his own thing on his own timetable. Dominic shook his head, thanking God this DVT hadn't put him in a nursing home. That would be nonstop care and other people meddling in his business. He didn't think he could take all that attention with no end in sight.

Pulling only a few feet into the driveway, he pressed

the button to roll down the window on the passenger's side. Bridget was the upside of round-the-clock care.

"Why are you standing on the lawn?" he asked Bridget's back.

She turned from whatever landscaping had caught and held her attention. "Why aren't you home?" she threw back at him. "For an invalid, you seem to get out quite a bit."

"I'm not an invalid," Dominic said. "Had to drive my daughter over to her boyfriend's house."

"You got a kid that young?" Bridget asked, hand firmly planted on hip. "I thought you'd raised yours."

"She's past thirty...but it's complicated, you gotta know how it is. He popped the locks. "Get in."

Bridget opened the passenger door with some effort and hopped into the passenger seat. Dominic tapped the accelerator and drove the truck thirty feet into the garage.

"Short ride," she said, getting out of the truck before he could make his way over to help her.

He pressed a button on his keychain to close the heavy wood garage door. Bridget followed him up the walkway. He sorted through Nick's keys, Adonis', and Gemma Hart's before finding the coil that held his.

"That's a lot of keys."

"Kids. Jobs. Cars." He'd pushed the brass into the lock when he remembered something. "Speaking of cars, where'd you park? You need a permit to be here after six. Too many residents and not enough spaces. I can find you one of those visitor hang tags."

Bridget cleared her throat. She looked at her toes as

she shifted from one sparkly foot to another. "I...uh...got a ride."

Parking enforcement issue solved, Dominic turned the well-oiled lock and pushed in the door. Zoe had been right. The smell of garlic was strong. He turned and led Bridget through the back vestibule, past the washer and dryer. "Seems like a lot of people need rides these days. What's your excuse? You're too young to have given up driving. Your kids didn't pull your license, did they? I hear that happens to old people these days."

"Ha, Dominic Andreis. You're a sly one. I promise I'm not a day older than you. Truth is, I never liked driving much. I try not to do it if I don't have to. One less driver on the road is the best thing that could happen to this city."

"Amen to that. Have a seat. Sorry for the mess. Mind keeping me company while I clean up?" He gestured to the sturdy square table in the corner of the kitchen. "Do you use one of those ride shares or taxis?"

"Can't afford anything fancy like that. My kids are happy to carry me around."

It took nearly all his willpower to bite his tongue. He couldn't imagine too many kids that wanted to cart their able-bodied parents through Los Angeles traffic. "Both boys?"

"Yep. Cameron and Ryan. Great kids. Cameron's in LAPD. Vice unit. Ryan's a lawyer at Equia."

Boys.

That explained it. The relationship Iris'd had with his boys had been close. They'd have laid down their lives for her. For him, not so much. He still loved them anyway.

Dominic peeked in the warming drawer that Adonis had insisted on. Seemed stupid at the time they were renovating the kitchens in the two-family. But resale value was everything around here, so he'd done it. Had to admit there was something nice about keeping food warm. He looked at Bridget's trim figure in the magenta tracksuit. The fabric looked like it would be really soft to touch. He shook his head. Damn, she was nice looking, thin though. She probably ate like a bird.

"You hungry by any chance?" he asked, mostly to be polite. Nine times out of ten in Los Angeles, women said no to that question even if their stomachs were rumbling loud enough to shake the birds out of trees.

"I was hoping you'd ask. It smells really good in here. What did you make?"

Relieved he wouldn't have to eat while being stared at, Dominic slid two platters from the warmer.

"Zoe and I made squid, octopus, sardines, and lemon potatoes. She wanted to cook for her guy. But she says I have an old world touch she can't match."

Bridget scrunched up her nose. Dominic didn't miss the movement. "I guess I shoulda asked. Do you like seafood?"

"I'm not sure I've had any of that before. Except potatoes. Of course I've had potatoes."

"You've probably had calamari, right?"

"Yeah. Sure. But you didn't say that."

"Squid. We call it *kalamarakia.*"

"So no marinara sauce?"

"You sound like Iris. She would drown…" He hadn't read a single book about 'getting back out there' or had time to cruise the internet for advice 'dating for the older set,' but opening with the wife had to be a no-no.

Dominic turned away from Bridget's earnest gaze and got back to the food. He pulled a serving bowl from the cabinet, and lined it with paper towels. He put all the fried squid in the bowl. Bridget's eyes widened.

"Hold on. It gets better." He went out into the back-yard and picked a few ripe lemons from the tree. Came back in and sliced one on the cutting board. "No allergies, right?"

Bridget watched him with an eagle eye. "Nope."

Shielding her from the spray, he squeezed lemon juice on the squid. "*Kalí óreksi!*"

"What's that mean in English?"

"Enjoy your meal. *Bon appétit*? Good eating. Something like that."

Bridget sat, her hands primly folded in her lap.

"Crap. You need a fork." He turned back to the cutlery drawer. Glad he'd minded his manners and not picked up one or two rings with his fingers. Napkins, forks, knives, spoons in hand, Dominic placed all on the table as neatly as he could.

"You want something to drink? Wine. Water. Ouzo?"

Not as hamstrung by manners, she picked up a golden ring. "Mmmm. This is really good."

Bridget's eyes were closed. Her lips glistened with olive oil. Dominic felt something stir below. Nope, he wasn't dead down there. He'd thought so for a long time, but not anymore. 'It's alive,' he wanted to crow like Dr. Frankenstein. He glanced down at his grampa shoes and tights. Damn. Nothing said 'great catch' like lady tights.

"Okay without marinara?"

"More than okay." Bridget looked him up and down. He tried not to fidget. *Don't look at the shoes, don't look at the shoes,* banged around in his head. "Sit down. I can't eat when someone's hovering around."

"Let me make you a plate. A little bit of everything, okay?"

"If it's this good. Sure."

He made two plates, handing one to her and placing the other opposite. Clearing the crowded table, he moved the rest of the squid to the shelf under the heat lamps. "You catching a ride home?"

"You trying to get rid of me already?"

"Not at all. But if we don't have to drive, I vote for ouzo."

"Why not?" Bridget said, like having a sip of alcohol was throwing caution to the wind. This one needed loosening up. He was just the guy to do it. Moving to the cabinet over the fridge, he wrapped his hands around the small clear bottle. The navy-bordered cream label was slightly rough under his palm just like it had been the first time he'd held his first bottle on his eighteenth birthday. Mentally, he tried to shake the memories from his mind. This was not the time to take a trip down memory lane.

Plunking the bottle on the table, he retrieved two tall shot glasses as well.

"Have you had ouzo before?"

"No. Never."

Dominic eased the cork from the bottle and poured himself a full glass. For Bridget, he filled it halfway. Then he filled it to the brim with water. He handed her the glass of newly cloudy liquid. She threw back half the drink in the blink of an eye.

No cough.

No tears.

Just a smile.

He was going to have to think about her 'no' and 'never.'

"How do you like it?"

"Pretty good. Great with the food. What's the rest again?"

Dominic cut the octopus with kitchen shears into bite sized pieces as he named everything on their plates. He took less than a mouthful of the ouzo while Bridget took a tiny bite of the mollusk. Bridget's next bite was more generous. Then she added more lemon and took a fourth bite.

"You like it? Try the potatoes. They were my mother's specialty."

"It's all really good. Takes a load off my shoulders. Your daughter said something about cooking dinner before giving you meds."

It all came together in his head in that moment. "Damn. Did she now? I thought everyone was just church social friendly all of a sudden. Now I know why I have a deep freezer full of casseroles."

Bridge finished her ouzo. "That's really good. I've never had anything like it."

Dominic poured her another half glass then only got halfway out of his seat before she laid a hand on his arm. "No need to water it down this time."

"Sip it a slowly this time, okay?" he directed before

filling the thumb sized glass to the top.

"When did your wife die?"

Dominic took a stuttering breath. It wasn't the punch in the gut it had been the first or second time someone had asked, but thinking of those days, weeks, and months that led up to his wife's death still took his breath away. Ignoring his own admonition to Bridget, he took a large sip of his own drink.

"Nearly twenty years ago. Ovarian cancer. We thought she'd pulled her back lifting some cabinets. When she didn't get better, the doctors kept renewing prescriptions for strong painkillers. After she lost about thirty pounds, we got a second opinion. But it was too late by then."

"So sorry to hear that," Bridget said after a suitably appropriate silence. "Did your kids think you should sue the doctor?"

"They were too young to think about things like that. Do your kids think you should sue someone?" Dominic asked because lawsuits weren't a random thought.

"Strohmeyer." Bridget refilled her own glass and took a small sip. "Ryan does at least."

"He's the lawyer, right?"

Bridget nodded. Added another potato to her plate. "My husband died in a work accident. They didn't pay more than a tiny life insurance policy. Ryan thinks I should have been set for life."

"At least you got his retirement, right?"

Placing her fork on her plate, Bridget shook her head. "The company declared bankruptcy or something and all the pensions were wiped out."

"Bankruptcy. That brewery's been chugging along

for all the years I've been here. I see steam puffing from those smokestacks every time I drive up north for work."

"I don't think it's bankruptcy like it would be for you and me where we'd have to sell everything and end up with nothing more than the clothes on our backs. It was some kind of business bankruptcy where they ditch their debts and pay shareholders a crapload of dividends."

"That kind of sucks."

"Yeah well. The Strohmeyers have a stadium named after them and more money than God. I have a leaky roof."

"What's wrong with it?" Dominic asked, leaning further forward. Rich people he couldn't do a damned thing about. Nailing tar paper to wood, he could handle.

"Nothing me or one of the boys can't fix," she said unconvincingly. He wondered who'd climb the ladder, the lawyer or the vice cop. His money wasn't on either. In the next minute, Bridget finished off her third or fourth glass, he'd lost count. She plopped it on the table with a resounding thud, then tried to wipe her mouth with the back of her hand in a way that wasn't obvious. "I've said too much. I didn't come here hat in hand. I came to help you. Tell you what. Why don't you take off those shoes and put your feet up in the living room. I'll wash the dishes."

Before he could protest, Bridget rose to her feet. She was only the tiniest bit unsteady. Someone who hadn't seen her put away that ouzo may have guessed that she had tripped on a groove between the wide planks on the floor. But he knew better.

"You should take a load off. I can get this," he said, chivalry getting the better of him.

"Nope. Your daughter was quite clear. Plus from the sound of it, you've been driving today. That's extra reason to get those feet up there. Don't make me chase you. Go watch football or something. I'll be back here in a few shakes of a lamb's tail."

As soon as her back was turned, Dominic took a rag from a bin in the kitchen and made himself scarce. He wouldn't put it past Bridget to report back to Zoe. Incurring the wrath of his favorite daughter was low on his list. Before he got cozy with the couch, he walked down the hall to the master bedroom. Carefully, he re-taped the plastic sheeting from the top of the door to the bottom.

He'd hated seeing Zoe's disappointed face when she'd kicked plaster dust off her shoes. He'd done the best he could keeping their Chicago house together after Iris had left...died. But between running a construction business full time and trying to raise three children, it had been hard. Maybe he'd been more ambitious in home improvement projects than he could realistically handle.

Admittedly, the kitchen being torn apart for a year and a half wasn't the best parenting. When the upstairs bathroom addition had gone awry after he'd discovered the rot in the walls, he'd nearly thrown in the towel and bought one of those new condos. Sharing a bathroom with a teenage girl had nearly sent him and the boys around the bend. But trying to keep the kids in the house they'd been in since birth had probably gotten in the way of good sense.

He'd tried to make it up to her with the glam teen

bathroom and customized bedroom, but his Zoe only seemed to remember the plaster dust in every crevice of her clothing, and eating microwave meals.

Resolved not to regret how he'd handled the kids, he stood up from taping and wiped the cloth along the baseboards in the hall, and again on the furniture in the living room.

Satisfied the house didn't look too much like a hardhat zone, he eased off his shoes, and the tights. The relief was immediate. The "Ahhhh" that escaped his mouth had been involuntary.

Drying her hands on a blue and white towel, Bridget poked her head in. "I heard that. Sounds like you maybe overdid it today."

"I only get one life. Time with my daughter was worth it. You done in there?"

"Got the dishwasher loaded. Pots and pans drying on the counter. If you tell me where the soap is, I'll start it."

Dominic patted the sofa next to him. "Join me."

"The soap first. Don't put off till tomorrow—"

"In the butler's pantry."

"The what?"

"That room between the kitchen and the dining room."

"I know what it is, but I haven't seen one outside of the big houses I used to clean."

"Okay. Sorry. I store the bulk stuff in there. No guy named Alfred, I promise. Should be a million little blue-green pods in the tall cabinet."

Bridget and the towel disappeared. "Got it," he heard her call out. A few seconds later, the whisper quiet sound of water on dishes became the background noise. "Where's the bathroom?" she asked from the hallway.

"Damn it all to hell," Dominic cursed under his breath. He'd been so busy taping that damned plastic, he'd forgotten why it was lifted in the first place. The hall bathroom was under construction as well. He'd started out replacing some of the original tiles. Of course there'd been termite damage, and the project had grown larger. "Hold on!" he called out.

Rising to his feet again wasn't as easy this late in the day. Gamely, he put his slippers on and met her in the hall.

"Saw that green bathroom. Out of commission."

"The master bath is fine, but..." Dominic unsealed the sheeting. "You'll have to step around the work. Just be careful. Holler if you need anything," he said before stepping out of the room to give her privacy. It was only when he got back to the couch that he realized he'd traipsed white dust back into the living room. He really needed to fix those coved ceilings. Gemma Hart being out in Malibu had made it damned difficult to get any of his own work done. The two plus hours in the car each day had eaten up all his free time.

"What did you settle on?" Bridget asked, sitting a respectable distance away on the couch.

Dominic rested the remote on the arm of the couch, careful not to put it between them in case she decided to slide a little closer. "This nine thousand inch screen came from the kids last Christmas. Somehow, they didn't think I was living life without some kind of LCD, LED, plasma, whatever. But now all I have is fifty-five inches of nothing to watch."

The tinkle of Bridget's laugh was like music to his ears. "Let me see that." Expertly, she took over the remote, scrolled through six hundred channels and landed on the opening scene to *Caddyshack*.

They laughed through the first ten minutes.

"I loved this movie when it came out," Bridget said. She pressed pause. "Hold on."

Five minutes later, she came back with a small plastic tray, bottle of ouzo and two clean glasses. Setting the tray on the sofa sized ottoman, carefully away from his foot, she sat much closer than the first time. Good thing that remote wasn't in the way.

For a long second, Dominic considered the yawn and stretch routine he'd perfected in his teen years. Nah, that was too juvenile even for him.

"Do you remember where you were when you saw this?" she asked during a lull in the action.

Closing his eyes, he thought back a long moment. The early eighties was a long time back. "I think someone volunteered to take the kids. It was only two kids back then, before Nicki. They were…probably still are…a handful. It was one of the first post kid dates I remember. We, Iris and I debated between this and *Airplane*. I like Chevy Chase better than Leslie Nielsen, so I won out. Still think I made the better choice, even now." Dominic stretched his arms toward the sky. One may have landed on the back of the couch behind Bridget. "The best thing I remember about this movie was getting in out of the heat. Chicago summers were brutal."

"Did you just put your arm behind my back?"

Busted.

Dominic was fifty-five, not fifteen. "I wanted to get closer to you. Is that a crime?"

"Maybe I should cuff you," Bridget said, her voice low. He was thinking about who would cuff who when a stranger's voice broke in.

"Ma? What in the hell is going on here?" The question came from a man who looked like he lived in Gold's Gym.

"Cam—"

"Am I going to have to arrest this old man for assault?"

THIRTEEN

Zoe

"Let me load the dishwasher at least," Zoe said, standing helplessly in the kitchen at odds for something to do.

"You slaved over a hot stove for hours. I'll wash up," Max said.

Zoe leaned against the counter. "I'd love to take the credit."

"That was the best meal I've had in a long time," Max threw over his shoulder. "The thought was yours," he said. He shut the appliance and pushed a few buttons. A loud whoosh filled the kitchen.

"At least we ate the food this time," she said, lowering her voice. The memory of that first time they'd skipped dinner fired up her insides. Dinner had been a bad, bad idea. Two long hours of eating and talking had separated her from what she'd really come here for.

"Um, right." Max stuttered out. Was he embarrassed?

Well, that was awkward. Getting from dinner to sex was proving a little harder than last time.

"Can I see your watch collection? You do have a collection, right?" she asked, deliberately dropping her voice an octave, aiming for the same tone a man would use when asking a woman to see his etchings.

An honest-to-goodness blush rose high on his cheekbones. But he didn't take her to the bedroom. Instead he said, "Sure, they're over here." Max gestured toward the desk and hutch that occupied the wide entrance hall.

From the antique looking wood furniture, he eased out a drawer. "Come closer," he beckoned.

She did what he asked, trying her hardest not to let the heady smell of the man get to her. Lightheadedness she'd wanted to attribute to anything but this moment made her brain swim a little. Closing her eyes for a second, she opened them again and focused on what he was showing her.

Like a museum that kept insect specimens in a drawer, Max had a glass-topped case that held about a three dozen watches. Each rested on a little stand like he had his own department store display counter in his house. But the watches were way more expensive looking than what you'd see at the counter in the mall.

"It's like you have a Rodeo Drive resale store in here. Is that a Rolex? Patek Philippe, Cartier? Geez. It's like Geneva's Rue du Mont Blanc in a drawer. That's amazing."

The blush continued to ride high on his cheeks. She wondered what he was embarrassed about. "These are the fully restored ones I wear." He pushed the drawer closed and pulled open another. "These are under construction."

The next drawer was divided into compartments with little gears, cogs, and teeny, tiny screws and a million other miniscule parts that probably added up to a watch with the liberal application of time and tools.

"Kind of cool," she said. Grabbing his hand, she pulled him in the direction of the bedroom. Like a mountain, he didn't budge.

"Let's try the living room," he said, tugging her in the opposite direction.

"C'mon you didn't invite me here to talk."

The blush that had only faded moments ago returned in full force. He sat on the blue suede couch, pulling her down alongside him. "I like talking too."

Zoe laid her palms alongside his stubble roughened cheeks. "We've had two hours of talking. Talking is overrated." Leaning closer, she did what she'd wanted to do since the moment she got here.

Kiss.

Forget.

It was so easy to get lost in his kiss. Firm but yielding lips brushed against hers. The bristle of stubble stung at her cheeks. The juxtaposition of soft, hard, and friction was just enough to send a tingle to all the places that mattered. Restless, she shifted just enough to push him off balance.

His head hit the cushion a second before her chest connected with his. Her nipples rubbing against her bra ratcheted up her anticipation. Making no bones about her intentions, she ground her hips against the erection she could feel not-so-gently pulsing against her.

She pulled her lips from his and hesitated while she tried to decide if she wanted to unbutton his shirt first or go right for the belt buckle that was keeping another unnecessary layer of fabric between them. She'd popped two buttons from their stricture when she heard the rumble of words come from the chest under her fingers.

"Stop."

"Stop what?" she asked. Her voice sounded huskier than usual to her own ears.

His green-gold eyes pinned her in her place. "Overwhelming me before I get a chance to look at you. Appreciate you. Pleasure you."

"You don't have to—"

"No, but I want to."

It was Zoe's turn to blush. She could feel the heat warming her face. Confidence had never been her issue. But scrutiny from the opposite sex was hard. She didn't want to be found wanting. Too tall, small tits, not enough shampoo commercial hair were her known deficits. Aware of her limitations, she'd learned to get a guy so far gone, he wasn't thinking about whether she could sweep his whole body with her hair. Max was easily silenced with a single kiss. Hand firmly on the leather around his waist, Zoe held his head with one hand and worked to get his pants off with the other.

"Zoe, stop," Max commanded. He pushed up on his elbows, then propelled them both to sitting. "I want to get to know you better in more ways than one."

"What do you want to ask me?" she asked, her question ending on a sigh her father would have called petulant.

"It's not anything specific. I want to know more about you."

"I wear a thirty-four 'B' bra. You want to see it?"

"That's not exactly what I was aiming for."

"From what I can see you aren't aiming at anything," Zoe said, grazing a hand down the bulge straining at the zipper of his jeans. "I'd like you to aim my way."

"Damn, I promised myself we wouldn't do this," he said to himself more than to her.

"Wouldn't do what?"

"This."

He pushed her back on the couch this time.

This.

This is what she wanted.

This is what she came for.

It wasn't the fish or potatoes or antique stuff. It was him that she wanted. Him that she'd come for.

Max didn't ask anymore. He took.

She was happy to give it all to him. Their hands collided as her tank was shoved up, then off. Her jeans came next. His mouth crashed onto hers. Large, sure hands covered her breasts. Imagining those hands capable of driving a bus, then crafting a watch ratcheted up her arousal. Zoe's heart slammed into her ribs, then the pulsing moved to her stomach, then further below. She squirmed under his hulking frame, wanting so much more. As if he could read her mind, Max moved his hand down and stripped her bare.

A single deliberate finger landed on her clit. Then she

was flying. It was like an out of body experience watching him pleasure her with single-minded determination. If he was this good with his hands, it was no wonder he was able to put those watches back together. That was her last thought before she came apart. She only hoped he'd be able to put *her* back together later.

Gently, Max kissed her calf, her knee, her most sensitive spot where his thumb had only left moments ago, her hip bone, the underside of her breast, a freckle that dotted her chest, then her lips.

"Do you want—"

He caught her hands in his. Though he wasn't more than a few inches taller than her, Max's hands dwarfed hers. "Not now. Talking first. More later."

"I'm underdressed for this conversation, can we do it in bed?"

"Not falling for that," Max said. He disappeared and returned a moment later with the robe she'd borrowed during her first visit to his house. "Here."

"What are you so fired up about? What do you need to know?"

"When are you going back to Europe?"

Zoe hid her now trembling hands into the voluminous folds of the terry cloth sleeves. "Soon. Why?"

Max curled a single finger under her chin. "We're kind of involved here. I'd like a heads up when you're ready to disappear from my life."

"I wouldn't disappear on you. I'd say goodbye at the airport like a normal person."

"So it'll be goodbye?"

"Max. Please don't do this. I live in Europe. You live

in the States. Not only the States, but the farthest west you could be. I'm in the middle of the continent on the other side of the earth. In a few weeks, six thousand miles will separate us. I've never lied to you about that."

"What if I want more?"

Zoe closed her eyes for a long second. Why was he making this so damned complicated? "Great sex and a love of continental cuisine is all that we have, Max. A fling. I'm loving this right now. You're the perfect respite from family, illness, and rehabilitation. Why can't that be enough?"

It was his turn for his lids to come down. The eyes that reminded her of a leopard about to pounce broke their stare. When his eyes opened again, she knew what was coming. She may not be a mind reader, but the hairs on the back of her neck stood on end. "Is your brother the reason you won't stay in Los Angeles?"

"I don't talk about this, Max," she warned.

"I overheard all of you arguing in the lobby at the hospital," he continued as if she hadn't spoken.

"This falls under the category of 'off limits.'" This time she made sure there was finality and closure in her voice.

"Did he really kill someone?"

Zoe wasn't answering that. Turning her back on him, she stood and fished through her backpack on the floor. Retrieving her phone, she checked to see if any messages had come through about her father. The badges above all the apps were mercifully missing.

Only a few e-mails from friends, and people at the syndicate graced her inbox. She turned around, pointing the blue light of the phone toward him. Sometime in the last few hours, the room had grown noticeably darker.

"It's getting late. Can we go to bed? I promise I won't even jump your bones."

Light from the moon or a streetlight glinted off the small area of Max's chest that she'd managed to expose when she'd been trying to get him naked. Slowly, he rose from the couch.

"Bed it is. We'll need to get an early start."

Relieved that he'd dropped the subject of her brother and her imminent departure, she lifted her backpack and made a beeline for his bathroom.

She'd forgotten a toothbrush, but she borrowed Max's. That little bit of intimacy made her feel that much closer to him. His question reminded her that she'd soon be on a huge jet putting six hundred miles per hour of distance between them.

Emerging from the bathroom, Zoe tossed the robe on the window seat and crawled under the covers while he did his own nightly thing in the bathroom. She was already half asleep when he lifted the duvet. Sliding under the covers he curled around her. The boxers he'd kept on did nothing to hide his arousal.

Turning, she smoothed her hands along his chest, then down to his hips, drawing off the cotton. Even if nothing more happened, sleeping was better when there was little between them.

♥

Dominic

"How'd you get in here?" Dominic stood as quickly as his legs would allow. He gripped the back of the couch hard, making sure not to let the stockings slip on the wood floor.

"You left the front door unlocked. No one answered when I knocked," Bridget's son said as if Dominic were in the habit of inviting axe murderers to break bread.

"I'm snug as a rug in a bug. No, wait. I'm as bug as a snug. Damn." There was an unmistakable slur in her voice.

A finger pointed at his chest. "Did you get my mother drunk?" To Bridget, Cam said, "How much have you had to drink?"

"I'm a grown woman who had a little ouzo."

"You're not fit to drive."

"I don't drive. You're here to pick me up, remember. Now I'll just go use the little girl's room, and we can get going." Bridget said, walking down the hall. With the TV muted and not a word shared between Dominic and this burly cop of a son, the sound of plastic sheeting being moved crackled through the apartment.

"You must be Cameron. I can't thank you enough —"

"What are your intentions?"

For a moment, he was transported back to his nine-teen-year-old self, standing on the stoop of Iris' childhood house. "This is only the second time someone's asked me that question," he started. But he wasn't that scared teenage boy. He'd run away once, and almost lost the girl. Age gave you gray hairs, and creaky knees, and more doctor visits than you could stomach. But it also gave him the wisdom not to make the same mistakes. "I like your mother. I plan to see her again if she's interested."

He must not have heard Bridget coming back, but he heard her voice loud and clear. "I'd really like that."

Ninety nine percent of people must back down when Cameron pointed his finger, because he looked surprised at the both of them. Dominic worked hard not to let the elation filling him with Bridget's words, melt the stern look he was trying to keep on his face. "It was nice meeting you, Cameron. Can you please step outside so I can say a proper good bye?"

The boy's eyes shifted first to him, then his mother, then back to Dominic. Unblinking, Dominic stood his slippery ground. Without a word, the cop turned and walked back out the door he'd barged through.

They were alone like he'd wanted, but Cameron had left an awkward silence in his wake.

"Thanks for babysitting me. I hope you enjoyed the food and the drink." The words tumbled from his mouth before he could think better of it.

Bridget moved closer, her approach on those sequined flats as quiet as a pouncing cat.

"I meant what I said back there," Dominic started again while she moved ever closer. "It would be nice to maybe go for a dinner or a movie. I hear that the Arclight is good. Reserved seating and all that—" Bridget was close enough to grasp both sides of his polo shirt and pull him close. Before he could remember the next words, he was planning to say, her lips landed on his. In that moment Dominic didn't give a crap about movies or dinner. For the first time in a long time, he felt alive.

FOURTEEN

Max

"So how does this work?" Zoe asked, barely stifling a yawn.

The ride from his place to Pasadena had been quiet. He half suspected she wasn't looking out the window, but dozing.

"You're not a morning person?" he asked. Heat snaked up his neck and he was glad for the green light on Orange Grove. He'd meant for them to get some sleep last night after he'd put on a clean pair of prophylactic boxers. But the temptation of her eager lovemaking had overridden his common sense for another time.

"I'm not sure anyone outside of an agrarian economy is a morning person. No cows to milk and access to coffee freed us from sunrise being our alarm clock," she said, letting him off the hook. It wasn't that he was embarrassed by sleeping, or *not* sleeping with her. It was just that he usually had a lot more control around the opposite sex.

"There's a coffee and pastry stand right behind the

gates," he offered after she held the back of her hand against her mouth once again.

"Thank goodness for small favors. I can't believe you don't have a coffee maker in your house."

He followed the signals of men and women in reflective jackets, parking on the lawn on the east side of the stadium. Zoe looked around, her eyes wide with amazement. "There are thousands of cars here. I thought this wasn't a morning town. New York City has bankers running around at the crack of dawn, but here Beverly Boulevard is empty until noon."

"It isn't any busier than usual," he said.

"There isn't even a game. No USC versus UCLA or whatever, and still this place is almost completely full. These people are all here for used stuff?"

"That they are." He turned off the car and pocketed the keys.

"Wow. I don't think I'll ever understand L.A.," Zoe said, unbuckling herself.

"Surely you must have had something like this where you grew up." Max opened his door. He was around the car as quickly as he could, but she'd opened her door before he could do it for her.

"Chicago? I guess there was Maxwell Street when I was a kid. We sometimes went there to see what kind of old toys and books were around. But we didn't get there at the ass crack of dawn."

They followed the streaming crowd to the temporary ticket booths.

"Maxwell Street? I've been there. Although I couldn't

figure out why it was called the Maxwell Street market when there was no Maxwell Street in sight."

"Yeah, well. The story is the same anywhere in America, right? Developers moved in and the market had to move out. Did you find anything there?"

"Can't remember that. I was there for a weekend. Took in a Cubs game, the Art Institute, and the market."

At the front of the line, Max asked for two tickets to the swap meet. He slid over a fifty before Zoe could extract her wallet from the overstuffed backpack. The least he could do was pay her way. It's what men did.

"Let me give you this," Zoe said, handing him some money.

He looked at the head on the oddly sized bill. The billowing hair and bushy moustache didn't resemble the founding fathers of the U.S. "I don't think I can spend this."

Zoe looked back at him, dragging her eyes from the temporary outdoor café menu and glanced at the money. "Sorry. Five hundred forint won't go far here."

"How much is that in dollars?"

She shrugged. "Maybe a buck fifty? I could buy coffee and a pastry with money to spare back home." She took the pink bill and tried to jam it into the overstuffed wallet. "Damn, I've got too many bills in here, but I didn't know which countries I'd go through."

"What else do you have in there?"

"Euros, Pounds, Forint. Probably a couple of Canadian bills in there too. I emptied out my money drawer before I finalized the flight reservations."

"What kind of coffee do you want?" Max asked,

changing the subject. He didn't want to think about her and reservations and international airports.

"I'll get this." Zoe had finally pulled green dollar bills from the wallet. "Two cappuccinos and what churros? When in Rome …."

Five minutes later Max watched her, his coffee cooling and his fried dough uneaten. He was kind of an egg man himself.

Zoe sunk her teeth into the fried dough pastry. "I was skeptical. Not quite the same as the ones I'd eaten in Spain, but not too bad. Cinnamon sugar and deep fried pastry made in a food truck. Who knew?"

"Let's go," Max said brusquely.

"Sorry, am I holding you back from the bargains?"

"Yeah, sure," he turned and stood with his back to the table, hands on hips. He'd lost control more times than he'd like to admit with her. It had been firmly back in his grasp when he'd woken up that morning. But seeing the bliss on her face, the pink tongue snaking out to capture the sugar crystals on her lips, that single act had nearly made him forget why he'd driven all the way to Pasadena. For a split second, he'd nearly chucked their tickets into the nearest bin, taken her back to the car, and violated some decency laws.

A light tap landed on his shoulder. "Ready," Zoe said. When she'd situated her backpack over both shoulders, he gave in to his desires a little bit, leaned forward and kissed her just a hint too long given the swirling eddy of people around them.

Dusting off her shorts, Zoe looked at him from under

her lashes. "Is there a map or something? Where are the watches?"

"I think they used to have a map. But things are grouped together kind of by type." He pointed to different sections of the vast parking lot outside the rose bowl. "There are clothes in one place. Food in another. Furniture is over there."

"I'll follow you."

He led her past the weapons. "That's something you see in Europe. Lots of World War Two and Cold War stuff," she commented.

"I thought you didn't go to swap meets."

"Not exactly. But almost every city I've been to has some kind of market like this. Maybe there they sell old and new? Lots of old books, Roman coins, war stuff. But there's usually a lot of handmade stuff too."

"I'd say this leans heavily on the used side."

They stepped over Persian rugs laid out on the asphalt. Zoe's husky laugh caught him up short.

"We buy junk. We sell antiques," she said, reading a sign painted on a piece of scrap wood.

"That about sums it up."

"Oh, my God. My denim jacket is turning over in its grave," she said. Max looked down to see a ten foot square blanket covered in buttons and patches.

CANOGA PARK

By Zöe Andreis

"There's something for everyone."

"Max. There's a guy selling watches. Are you going over?"

"Sure. Let me introduce you to Stan."

"Max Kiss. Are you kissing this lovely lady?" Stan took Zoe's hand and bussed the back in a courtly gesture. "I'm Stan, by the way. Your boyfriend is not one of my best customers. He gives Marcella over there all his business."

"This is because Stan refurbishes watches himself."

"Oh, this looks like the one you showed me last night," Zoe said, pointing to a Breitling Navitimer. To Stan she asked, "How much?"

"Seven thousand eight fifty. But for a pretty lady like you, a flat seventy five hundred."

"Seriously? At a flea market. You take credit cards?"

Stan held up a small plastic card reader. "Happy to."

"Not in my budget today," Zoe said. She extended her hand again. "Nice meeting you, though."

"Nice meeting Max's girlfriend." Stan held out a fist festooned with gold chain. Max fist bumped him reluctantly. He had never been one for preening male displays.

They wandered back into the walkway between stalls. "He thinks you're my boyfriend. I haven't had a boyfriend since the twentieth century."

"Would it be so bad being my girlfriend?" Max asked.

"Is that Marcella?" she asked, pointing to the second watch stand in the quadrant, ignoring his question.

"Let's go see what she's got."

"Max. I wasn't expecting you today." She turned around to the back of the booth and dug through some cardboard boxes. "But I put something aside for you in case you're interested."

"You didn't give it to Stan?"

"That man gives me the willies with all that hand kissing and fist bumping." She plopped a muslin parcel in his hand. "Take a look. Tell me what you think."

Moving to one side of the display table, he pulled the twine from the fabric. Zoe leaned closer as the square of cotton fell open. Max's head nearly exploded. "What year is this, Marcella?"

"Nineteen fifty-eight was the best I could do."

Zoe looked back and forth between them. "Someone say something. What will this pile of metal turn into?"

"It's an Omega Speedmaster."

"Okay…"

"It's the watch that NASA astronauts used in space flight."

"That's cool. This one didn't go up in space though, right?"

"Those watches are probably in the Smithsonian. Marcella, how much do you want for this?"

"Two."

"Dollars?" Zoe asked.

"Thousand," Max answered.

Zoe stuck a single finger into the bundle. "It doesn't work, right?"

"But it'll be worth a mint once Max gets it fixed."

"This is out of my budget, Marcella."

"I worried you might say that, but I wanted to give you first dibs. Stan doesn't respect the history. I can't bear this Omega to become a Frankenwatch."

"You could fix it," he said to the seller.

Marcella held up fingers bent by arthritis. "I wish I could, but these hands gave out before the rest of me did."

"I tell you what, I'll think on it," he said, trying to work out in his head how he could pay for a nurse and the object of his desire.

"You have my number. Text me before noon. Otherwise I'll let you-know-who in on it."

"Great meeting you," Zoe said, cradling Marcella's hands between hers.

They moved on. "She was nice to do that for you. Why aren't you getting it? She made it sound like it was at the top of your must have list."

"It's outside my budget," Max said. "I *am* a bus driver. That doesn't leave me with a lot of spare cash in this city."

"How much will Stan sell it for when it's refurbished, or rehabbed or whatever?"

"Stan?" Max blew out a breath. "Probably six or eight thousand."

"But you wouldn't buy it and sell it yourself? Guarantee the authenticity of the parts or whatever?"

"I'm not in the business of commerce. I do it because I love it."

"Hmmm. Okay," Zoe said, then went quiet.

They wandered around another couple of hours. Zoe's quick wit made him laugh out loud more than a few times. It was fun watching her mind work. He vowed in that moment when they passed yet another display of vintage movie action figures, new again because of one reboot or another, he'd get a subscription to the newspaper. When he couldn't wake up with Zoe in the same time zone, he'd love to peek into her world.

By Zöe Andreis

"You ready?" he asked when she started flagging.

"Sure. It was kind of tiring. I can't imagine what this would be like on a hundred degree day."

"Brutal," he admitted.

"I'd offer to make you lunch, but I'm all out of cooking creativity. I'll take you out, though. You pick the place, and do the driving."

"I'll take you up on that," Max said. But she was no longer next to him. He'd exited through the turnstile that barred reentry. Looking back, he saw her looking indecisive. "Do you mind if I run and get something for my dad? I swear I'll be quick. I think he'd love that Greek flag mug. Promise it won't take more than a minute.

Nodding, Max took a seat on an empty bench. Reluctantly, he took out his phone and tapped in Marcella's name. Her nine-four-nine number popped up on the display. Exhaling long and hard, he let her know he wouldn't be able to buy the watch. It was number one or two on the list of watches he'd always wanted to own, but he couldn't see a way he could afford it.

A few weeks ago, he'd have purchased the parts no questions asked, and figured out another way to economize. The reality of the situation with his father gave him pause. Hobby money would have to be reallocated to a part-time caretaker. Max rolled his head, relieving the tension that had built up at the mere thought of his father.

"Let's do lunch!" Zoe said after she emerged from the crowd. Her voice was full of laughter, lifting his mood. There'd be another watch on another day. This one wasn't meant to be.

"I'm not sure I've ever heard anyone in Los Angeles actually say that."

"I'm the first then," she said, bumping his hip with hers. She reached for his hand as if it were the most natural thing in the world. "What do you have in mind?"

"There's a Mexican restaurant that's nearly one hundred years old," he offered. Europe was full of old things. She seemed to like that.

"Right up my alley. Let's go!" She swung their joined hands back and forth. He'd always loved coming to the market, but doing it with a willing girlfriend was way better.

"Your backpack is ringing," he said after the faint ring-tone penetrated through the haze of lust that surrounded him.

"What? Oh, hold on a second." She pulled her hand away and he immediately missed the contact.

Women confused him with their sack like bags. Watching her search through the bag, was like watching her mine for gold. By the time she'd retrieved the phone from her bag, the ringing had long stopped. "Let's go to the car. I can call back from the road."

While he navigated the Toyota through the shady tree-lined Pasadena streets toward Old Town, Zoe's tapping at the phone grew more frantic.

"What's wrong?"

"My dad left a message saying he needed me. But he's not answering his phone. I have no idea if it's an emergency."

He looked at his watch. "We can be there in twenty-five minutes tops."

"I don't want to ruin your Sunday. It's just that my brother is out of town. I really thought everything would be fine for a few hours. He seemed so happy yesterday, planning a date night with Bridget and all that. Oh, God. I wonder if something went wrong with Bridget. One old person watching another wasn't the best idea. What was I thinking?" Zoe continued to berate herself under her breath.

"What's the address?" he asked, making an executive decision to alter their Sunday plans.

"What?"

"Your dad's address? He's in the city, right?"

"It's North Orange Drive, near Beverly and La Brea." She tapped at the phone. "Do you need directions?"

Max's laugh was purposefully dry. "Um, no I think I've got it."

"Right. The bus. Sorry. I forgot for a moment. I'll just shut up now."

FIFTEEN

Zoe

Zoe strained her ears the moment they exited the Hollywood Freeway and made their way to Beverly Boulevard. Every bird chirp and horn beep sounded like the beginning of a siren's wail. Cell coverage had been spotty on the freeways or her father wasn't answering, not that he did under the best of circumstances. Every mile closer to Dominic's had her imagining the worst. Had he fallen? Had another clot let loose, causing a stroke? Would he be paralyzed for the remainder of his days?

When Max made the right hand turn, North Orange Drive was as quiet as always. The ficus trees barely moved. The sidewalks were bare of dog walkers and joggers. Not even a toddler on a tricycle graced the street. It took all the willpower in the world not to jump out of the car before he'd pulled into the driveway and to a complete stop.

No stretcher, gurney, or ambulance rolled down the sloping drive. A single taxi-yellow van was pulled up to the garage door. Absently she wondered if she'd seen that van before. Must belong to her dad's tenants or someone they knew.

"You going to be okay?" Max asked.

"I don't know," Zoe answered, wondering if her erratic breathing had been as loud for him as it'd been for her. "This is so out of the blue. I'd been feeling a lot better since I got here. I made a chart. I organized care. But it's like I'm back at square one frantically hoping my dad won't die while I can do nothing but stare down at the melting icebergs in the northern Atlantic from thirty-seven thousand feet."

"Let's go, then," Max said, shutting off the engine and pocketing his keys with a certain finality. "I'm learning it's better to face things head on."

"Oh, God. I dragged you out here. I'm so sorry. You don't have to come in. My family drama is enough for me. I had no plan to rope you into this."

"I'm here. C'mon."

Zoe didn't know if time had slowed or if she was the one moving like molasses. She closed the car door, took a deep breath, then made the walk to the door. She knocked as hard as her fist allowed.

"Papa!" she called. "You okay in there? I'm going to use my keys if you don't answer."

Silence greeted her. Zoe pressed her ear to the door, but couldn't hear anything through the solid fir her dad had talked about ad nauseum. Slipping the key ring from an outer pocket, she sifted through the unfamiliar keys. She landed on what she thought was the right one and inserted it into the dead bolt. It turned smoothly. The bottom lock wasn't engaged and she was able to open the door in one motion.

"Papa!"

"Back here!" he yelled.

Zoe dropped her bag by the door and hightailed it to the bedroom. Expecting to see one thing, but seeing something entirely different, it took a moment for it all to compute. Her father on a ladder with scraper in hand. Her brother Adonis bracing either side with his hands.

"What in the hell is going on? No one's dying. No one's in the hospital. And this is the second time I've found you on a ladder when you're supposed to be taking it easy."

"Pass me that smoother, will ya?" Her dad pointed in the direction of a table full of tools.

"You didn't answer my question, Papa."

"I'm fixing the coving."

"The what?" Zoe asked. Just when she thought she'd heard every construction term, there was one more that was unfamiliar.

Her dad looked at her as if she'd fallen off the turnip truck only moments ago. "The curved area above the molding. I know how you hate unfinished projects. I wanted to show you I'm not going to let this one go on for years. I can finish long before you board a plane back to Budapest."

Her dad pointed to a spot in the ceiling whiter than the rest.

"See this is the last little patch? I'll prime and paint it as soon as it's dry, then finish the room. I'm thinking an ocean blue. I have a color fan down there if you have something else in mind. You're the artist."

"You called me over here to see your ceilings?" To her brother, she said, "Adonis, how can you help him with this? I'm pretty sure curved ceilings aren't on his recovery plan."

"Coved, Zoe, not curved," Adonis corrected.

"I'm Max Kiss, by the way. We haven't met formally," her lover said, taking that moment to extend his hand as if they were all at a cocktail party.

"Adonis Andreis." Her brother took the hand and shook.

"Great, everybody knows everybody," Zoe said, looking around exasperated. She threw up her hands. "You're not dying. I'm outta here Papa. I'm not sure what in the heck is going on, but I don't want any part of this." To Max she said, "You ready for lunch?"

With a single noisy scrape against the flawless plaster, her father handed the tool to Adonis and stepped gingerly down the ladder. "Done. Don't go. You can eat here."

"No, Papa. I can't."

"When are you going to talk to your brother?"

"Didn't you hear me; I talked to him not a minute ago. I'm sure your hearing isn't the part of you that needs healing."

"If I have a dying wish, it's that you two start talking again," her father pleaded. He hunched his shoulders and cast his eyes down like he was about to place one foot in his own grave.

"I'm looking at you. You're walking and talking—not

dying. So, no wish granted. Maybe we'll revisit that when you *are* actually dying." Turning on her heel, she squeaked from the room, not caring about the plaster dust caking her shoes making tracks across the beautifully stained floor.

"Come back here Zoe Hestia Andreis! I'm talking to you."

"Hestia?" Max croaked. She'd forgotten he was there amidst the endless family drama.

"They went overboard with the Greek thing," she said to Max. "Adonis for example? Papa, I don't want to do this," she yelled over her shoulder as she retrieved her bag from the floor.

Her dad made it to the living room in record time. "If not now, when? I'm tired of my kids not talking. I'm tired of separate holiday celebrations. I'm tired, dear heart."

Zoe's chin dropped to her chest, her head weighed down by parental guilt. "What...do you want, Papa?"

"Talk to your brother. Patch up your differences."

"Differences? Are you serious? I don't see Adonis getting on a plane and beating down my door looking for reconciliation." Zoe looked at her oldest brother for the first time in a long time. Adonis looked everywhere but at her. "He can't even look me in the eye, Papa. He's a stone cold coward."

She watched Dominic look between them. First at her, then her brother, then back again like he'd done when they were all kids and it was time to kiss and make up.

"I'm sorry," Adonis croaked out.

It took everything in Zoe's power for her to choke down the sob that threatened to drown her. She didn't want to be so easily swayed by emotion. "Well, that's a good eleven years too late."

"Zoe!" Dominic's rebuke was sharp.

"Did you ever apologize to Emily's parents? I'm not the person you need to be apologizing to."

"They refused to speak with me after the trial." Her brother's voice was soft. Years ago that voice, accompanied by a suitable amount of guilt, would have been enough for her to forgive him. But it couldn't be that easy. Zoe wouldn't let him off the hook with a smile and some nice words. She took a deep breath, hardening her heart.

"Not shocking. You got away with murder."

"Is that what you really think? That I murdered your friend."

"Let's see, you drank, you drove, she died. I'm not sure which part isn't murder. I don't know why we're talking about any of this. The past is dead, and Emily is buried. Is this what you wanted, Papa? Is this how you imagined our grand reconciliation would be?"

"Your brother didn't go to jail, but he did his penance."

"What? Living in Oxnard is now penance? You should tell that to the guys at San Quentin. I'm sure they'd trade you."

"He goes to A.A. Has for ten years," her father said, pleading his case. He sounded just like the defense attorney he'd hired with the bulk of their family's savings.

"But he's living, and Emily is dead. She can't sit in a church basement eating stale cookies. Ever."

Zoe didn't know if the shaking that overtook her body was from anger at her brother or adrenaline as her body readied itself for flight. No matter how hard she tried to fight it, she couldn't keep the tears at bay. Giving in, she plopped down on the couch and let her hands hold up her head.

Strong arms came around her, holding her close. Holding her tight. Keeping her from splitting apart.

Max.

He made her feel better and worse all at the same time. She'd forgotten he was here, and now he'd seen her and her family at their absolute rock bottom.

"I'm sorry," she whispered to Max. "We should go. I had no idea we were walking into this."

"Don't apologize."

Zoe looked around for something to wipe her face and nose. For the first time she wished she were one of those women with a bucket of cosmetics in a designer purse.

"Do you have…"

Max looked over his shoulder. She didn't follow his gaze. "Let me get you something. Hold on."

"Dear heart. I'm really sorry. You're here in California —Los Angeles even. Your brother's down from Ventura County. I only wanted to get you guys together. Get you to see reason."

Zoe turned to look at her father. The face she'd loved for so many years. "What have I been unreasonable about?"

"Forgiving your brother."

"What he did was unforgiveable, Papa."

"But we have to move forward. We can't stay locked in the past."

"Adonis wasn't the only one affected, you know."

"You mean the driving?"

"I haven't driven a car in years, Papa. The thought of it terrifies me. Every time I imagine myself behind the wheel, I nearly pass out. I haven't been to a single college reunion. Everyone looks at me like the girl who killed someone even though I didn't do it.

They look at me like someone who should have stopped her stupid older brother from driving. I never tell them that I was the one who was supposed to be sober. That I was underage and got stupid drunk at a party full of frat boys with an agenda. That my brother who thought he wasn't going to have to drive—did to keep me and Emily from ending up in some bad situation…"

Zoe ran out of steam. Her head was starting to hurt. Decades-old memories pressed at her skull.

"I gotta go, Pap. Maybe later. Not now." This time she walked through the door without stopping. She walked down the drive and took a left toward Beverly Boulevard. She wasn't sure what her plans were, but staying at her father's house wasn't among them. The endless stream of cars, and noise, and honking didn't bother her for once. She let the sound and smells wash over her. A few minutes after crossing La Brea, she found herself seated outside at El Coyote ordering a scratch margarita. If she couldn't drive, at least she could get plastered.

"Can I join you?"

Zoe looked up. Max. She'd all but forgotten he'd driven her there. Their leisurely morning seemed like a figment of her imagination, a memory from the distant past.

"Sorry I left you out in the cold."

"You were easy to follow even though driving and parking took longer than you moving on foot."

"Life on foot is often easier," she said. "You want a drink?"

Max signaled for the waiter. "Tecate. And can we have a *carne asada* burrito La Cocina style. Two plates, and a big knife?"

"Coming up," the waiter said. Chips and salsa appeared on the table along with the drinks.

Before she could drink more than a few sips of the salty-sweet concoction, or ask him why he'd need a knife, a burrito the size of a small dog appeared on the table.

"Je-sus. I'd totally forgotten about this. My friends and I used to split these L.A. burritos at least four ways when we came out," she said, watching Max cut the food in half. He added sour cream, guacamole, and *pico de gallo* to her plate. Lunch, dinner, and dessert stared at her from the plate. Despite the intimidating size of half of the late lunch, she dug in. Zoe was a good chunk in before she paused.

"You were hungry."

"More than I thought." She took a large fortifying sip. "Sorry about what happened—"

"Don't be sorry. Family is...complicated."

She lifted her glass in a toast. "Don't you know it."

Max's face turned serious. "I think there are a couple of things you should know about me."

A thousand things rushed through her head from STDs to rap sheets. Under her lashes, she took Max in. He didn't seem the type to have a record, or a disease. He seemed like the type to sit at home and use tiny tools on even tinier parts. It was something she could relate to. A solitary activity that kept your brain fully occupied and your mind off other things.

"I have a dad."

"I didn't think you'd sprung from a cabbage patch."

Max didn't laugh at her joke. Instantly, she regretted her levity. "Sorry. You were saying."

"Watching you and your dad makes me...I don't know...wistful."

"Is your dad alive? In California?" she asked while gesturing to the lime still in the top of his beer bottle. "I don't like to drink alone."

"He's up in his house in Santa Clarita. Safe and sound. But he's—"

Max's thought went unfinished. The phone he'd put on the table under his car keys vibrated across the metal table. After a few moments, the buzzing stopped, then started again.

"Maybe you should answer that."

He looked at the phone. Frowned. Picked it up. "Max Kiss."

The frown only deepened. He rose and paced the small courtyard. Whomever was talking on the other end didn't leave much room for response. Finally Max spoke. "I'll be there in...." He glanced at his watch, then looked toward the fabric overhead ".... thirty minutes tops."

"You need to go, so—"

"Come with me. I'll show you what I was going to tell you," Max said. She'd let him into her world. It was time she saw his.

SIXTEEN

Max

Thirty minutes on the dot was the time from the parking lot of El Coyote to the driveway of his father's house behind a car that was kind of familiar and not his father's.

"Where are we?" Zoe asked. Whether it was the margarita or the early start, he didn't know, but she'd fallen asleep a few minutes after they'd left the restaurant.

"My dad's house."

The adult protective services woman was out of his house like a shot.

"Mr. Kiss. You're going to have to do something about the situation with your father. The police were unable to reach you this time, so they called me. Your dad was wandering again. But this time he nearly got hit by a delivery truck. The driver stopped at the last minute. He's quite shaken up."

"Good afternoon," he said, trying to remember the social worker's name. He offered his hand. Kathi McNabb

—the name came back to him in an instant—ignored the proffer. "Who's shaken up, my father or the driver?"

"The driver. He says he's been making deliveries to this neighborhood for over ten years, and has never come this close to hitting a resident."

It took all of Max's restraint to keep his mouth shut. He'd love to list the dozens of times he'd seen that boxy white and blue truck drive through the neighborhood ignoring the speed limit laws with impunity. His father wasn't the first person who'd probably dodged the driver. The kid in white shorts who liked to listen to blaring loud music, tap at his phone, and do everything but put his hands on the steering wheel with the same frequency he had his foot on the gas pedal.

"I'm Zoe Andreis," she said, coming from where she'd been standing next to the car. He noticed Zoe didn't offer her hand to Kathi.

"Are you the girlfriend?"

Zoe looked from him to Kathi and back. "Sure. Okay. Where's Max's dad?"

"He's inside. But I don't want him to get agitated with what I'm about to say."

"Go on," Max said, the dread of knowing full well what was coming settling into his bones.

"It's time to move your father to a more restrictive setting. I'm happy to provide you with a list of references for every budget." Kathy went to her trunk, popped it open, and extracted yet another folder. He'd throw it on top of the one she'd brought last week. He wondered what the county budget was for glossy white folders. "There's also information on Medicare allowances and financial planning, and all the rest you'll need to get everything situated.

"Are you done?" Max said brusquely, not sure if he was angry at Kathi, his father, or himself.

"Not quite."

"I get it. Thanks for your help. I'll take it from here." Ignoring Kathi's fish mouth, he walked toward the front door, girding himself for what awaited him inside. Hand on knob, he turned it, but it didn't budge. He turned a little to the left, ready to put a shoulder into it, to relieve the door from sticking. It didn't budge.

"Mr. Kiss," Kathi said. "It's not quite that simple. We've opened up a file on you. I'm going to be your father's caseworker. I'll be making weekly visits to make sure he has adequate care."

"Weekly? Don't you have more serious cases to attend to?"

"This *is* serious, Mr. Kiss."

"It's Kiss, like 'wish,' Ms. McNabb."

"Sorry. Right. Sorry. I know this is a hard time, but your father's safety is our first priority. He's not safe now."

Max put his shoulder against the wood, and the door gave way this time. He was grateful that Ms. McNabb took the hint. The caseworker buckled herself into her car and backed out of the driveway and down her father's quiet street.

"Dad?" Max called out. He eyed the living room. Empty. Same for the bathroom and master bedroom. Finally, he came to the open back door and looked outside. His father was pacing the perimeter of the back-yard. "What are you doing?"

Max had completely forgotten about Zoe until his father zeroed in on her. "Is she going to take me to the police station again?"

"No, Dad. This is my friend," he said. With Zoe there, he took a look at the yard as it would look through the eyes of someone who had never seen it before. It wasn't a pretty picture. Somewhere along the line, his dad had become obsessed with saving water and had turned off the sprinklers. Tufts of wheat colored grass stiff as hay filled the yard. Tattered remains of the table umbrella flapped in the warm breeze. The chairs were askew.

He hadn't been thinking clearly. Selfishly, he'd wanted his own life. But he should have moved back home when his mother got sick. Maybe he could have helped her. Or even kept his father's dementia from accelerating so quickly.

"Can you get a ride back?" he asked an unusually quiet Zoe.

"Do you want me to leave?"

"Yes. No. I don't know Zoe," Max said, keeping one eye on her and the other on his father. "You're very lucky. You have your brothers, and a house full of family and friends willing to kick in to help your dad. I saw the chart on the wall. That's a lot of people. It's just me and Dad here."

"You don't have any relatives? Friends?" Zoe asked as if everyone came with a big loving family and hundreds of friends who cared about you.

"They were immigrants from an Eastern Bloc country. After they left not many others came out. For a good forty years, communication was pretty spotty. We took a couple of trips, but time and space put distance between us and them." That and the son they'd lost. That had turned them against the Soviet way of doing things. Turned them against the world behind the Iron Curtain. "So no on the family question."

"My grandparents came to Chicago from Italy and Greece. Even though we had a bunch of relatives who eventually came over, there was the bigger community too. Was there no Eastern European community here? How'd they end up here anyway?"

"It's not like New York or Chicago in that way. They came here sponsored by the local Rotary Club. A few members helped him finance his lease, and he opened his business. But they were from a small country. They kept to themselves. So, no on the friends front as well."

"I'm not on the schedule today. And my dad is clearly fine and dandy. I can stay with you. Help with whatever you need."

Max wanted to take the help. But he didn't want to get used to something that would only be temporary.

"You got any *kenyérszalonna*?" his dad asked during a pause in his pacing.

"It's—"

"I know what it is. Do you have it? I can slice it."

Max nodded. "In the kitchen. Found a place that imports it. He only wants Hungarian food these days. It's hard as hell to get."

Zoe disappeared into the house. Max pulled the wood table away from the shed and storage area. Unfolded the chairs. He lifted the tattered umbrella and tossed it in the storage area. He'd have to make a special call to municipal services to have that hauled away. His dad was shuffling toward the chairs like a character from a zombie movie when he stopped dead cold.

Right then it hit him.

He understood why it was so hard to make a decision about his dad. If he put his dad into a home, he'd never come out. Nursing homes were death sentences. Alzheimer's was a death sentence. Hell, life was a death sentence.

Zoe backed through the door with a tray in her hand. It was laden with thick slices of bread, sliced red onion, and the fatty bacon Hungarians called *kenyérszalonna*.

"*Köszönöm szépen. Csókolom*," his father said after she'd set the table with the food. Following up, he kissed her hand ceremoniously then sat to eat.

"That was perfect," Max said. "Thank you. I didn't expect —"

"My whole job is observing cultures. It would be really bad if I couldn't set a Hungarian breakfast table."

"You want anything?"

"That baby burrito was enough food for the next week or two. I may not eat before getting back on an airplane."

"I'll get some water," Max said. The woman he was falling for was already talking about leaving him. And his father would definitely leave him one way or another.

He watched his father, quiet, content, chewing quietly. He pulled two glasses down from the cabinet. But as he was about to fill them, the greasy film made him look twice. Peering into the cupboard, he noticed it was filled with clean and dirty dishes mixed together. Before he could close it and open another, a bug of some kind scurried out of sight into a crevice in the wood.

He's been so damned naïve. Picking up stakes and moving back home wasn't a solution. A part time nurse wasn't a solution. The next step couldn't be avoided no matter how much he'd like to pretend the last four years hadn't happened.

Max watched his father. Swallowing the lump that had formed in his throat, he pulled out his phone and called dispatch. He made an emergency request for family leave. He'd never thought he'd use those days. Not unless he had a wife and a new baby or something. But that dream seemed farther away than ever. He needed to settle things for his father's generation before he could even think about starting the next one.

SEVENTEEN

Dominic

"Give her some room, Dad," Adonis pleaded.

"She needs to forgive you," Dominic said.

"I've barely forgiven myself. Maybe it's a tall order for her."

"Ah, I hear you. But I'm jealous of all the guys at the lumber wholesaler. They talk about Thanksgiving and Christmas and grandkids. I only just got a grandkid. Iris is a peach, but I'd love to have the two of you at Nick and Holly's when turkey day rolls around."

"I don't feel comfortable, Dad. We've been through this. I do fine up in Oxnard. Speaking of which, I really need to get on the road, otherwise I'll be in my truck for the rest of forever."

"Fine. Help me finish getting this plastic down."

"Who's up next? Zoe hasn't given you a moment to yourself." Adonis scanned the dry-erase board his sister had set up. "Devil horns, funny," he said under his breath.

"I'm not twenty-five any more, but I'm not hard of

hearing. You have devil ears, Nick's hair's too long. If I wasn't a charitable man, I'd assume your sister was making fun of us."

"Let me get the shop vac from the truck," Adonis said on his way out the back door.

Careful not to track dust, Dominic stepped through the bedroom and pulled open one dresser drawer, then another. Bridget was up next in the rotation, and he wanted to look good this time. Not wanting to be caught rifling through his own clothes like a teenager nervous for a date, he hastily chose a knit V-neck top. Dark gray slacks from the closet were next. When he heard Adonis slam the door on his way back in, he called out, "I'll be in the shower!"

"You're dressed nice," his son said, looking a little too comfortable on the couch.

"I thought you had to beat the traffic," Dominic said, trying not to be pushy, but being pushy.

"Who's up next?" Adonis asked, cocking his head sideways to read the chart. "Who's…Bridget?"

"Ah, a parent of one of Nick's friends. She's filling in the slots when the young people are out doing their thing."

Adonis wasn't stupid. It took him all of five seconds to add two and two. "You like her." It wasn't a question.

"We'll see where it goes. Okay. Just getting to know her a little. Nice to talk to someone who's old and decrepit like myself."

"Dad you're hardly—"

"You know what I mean. Now get going before *you* get DVT from sitting a thousand hours in your truck. Thanks for your help here on the house and with Gemma Hart," he said, all put pushing his oldest son out the door. Couldn't get his kids to visit often enough on the one hand, then couldn't get them to leave on the other.

Ten minutes turned to twenty while Dominic paced. He wasn't going to mess up his nice clothes fooling with the hall bathroom. But he didn't want to throw on coveralls in case Bridget came early. Vowing not to check the time on the range or the microwave, or the mantel clock in the living room, Dominic still found himself face to face with the digital time staring out from his blue LED radio display in the bedroom. When did the world turn so time sensitive? When he grew up, time hadn't seemed to matter so much. He eased himself on the edge of the bed and looked up. He'd done a pretty good job on the coving. If the earth didn't shake in the next couple of days, it would be crack free and ready for primer.

The hippy-dippy folks at the paint store had said that blue would make him depressed. But he was thinking otherwise. It might be nice to be in a room that was cool and soothing. The red brown he'd picked when he'd moved in had seemed masculine and clubby, but he didn't much like it anymore. Too dark and depressing.

"They don't have burglars on this side of the hill?" Bridget asked.

Dominic stood so fast, he nearly slipped in his loafers. "You're here."

"In the flesh. Good thing I wasn't a serial killer."

"My son probably left it open. He was carrying his shop vac and a toolbox. I should have checked."

"You look nice. Trying to impress me?"

Caught out, Dominic didn't know what to say. He

resorted to the truth. "I was, Bridget Becker. Did it work?"

It was her turn to blush. She was really very pretty. Not an olive skinned beauty like his first wife, Bridget was an entirely different kind of creature. Then she smiled, something it looked like she did rarely. Her blue eyes lit up. The light sprinkling of salt in her hair glinted in the late afternoon sunlight. The rhinestone studs on her black velour jacket and pants winked. "I think it did, Dominic Andreis."

She joined him on the bed he'd neatly made up an hour ago. He wasn't sixteen anymore, but a woman and a bed did certain things to a man no matter what his age.

"I made dinner. Hope you're hungry."

"I brought my appetite this time. Still marveling over what you did with that fish. A far cry from the fish sticks I sometimes served the boys."

"Be still, my heart," Dominic said as he led her from the room and got himself on an even emotional keel. A hunger of another kind took over.

"What did you make?"

Dominic pulled a couple of dishes from the warmer. "Nothing as elaborate as last time. Some *tirokafteri*, hummus, a little *souvlaki*."

"What's the other?"

"Yogurt dip, olives, the usual."

"Not my usual. Do you have more of that drink?"

"No way am I facing your son after getting you soused. I chilled a bottle of Malagousia."

"Mala—what?"

Dominic pulled a glass from a rack and poured a small amount in the bowl. "Taste it."

Bridget took a hesitant sip, then another before finishing off the glass. "That's like nectar from the gods. Where did you get that?"

"My daughter brings me bottles. The Greeks were making wine before anyone else in the world. Trust me when I say we got it right. The French and the Italians... they have better marketing."

Bridget's laughter was delightful. She wasn't shy. In a moment after he'd refilled her glass, she tore a piece of pita and dipped it in one sauce, then another. "Do you know the way to a woman's heart?"

"No, but I can't wait to hear."

EIGHTEEN

Zoe

"You're doing the right thing," she said to Max as they sat in standstill traffic on the Golden State Freeway.

In a moment, the traffic eased and no sounds filled the car's interior other than a litany of commercials from a classic rock station.

"I'll drop you at your place," Max said, taking an exit and deftly weaving his way through traffic.

He was at her door in a heartbeat. She made no move to exit. "Are you coming in?"

"I shouldn't."

"Why not?"

She could practically see the internal debate raging on his face. Making the decision for him, Zoe eased the keys from the ignition and opened first her door, then his.

"I think you have this all backwards."

"No Max, I don't. In a couple not all the comfort goes one way. C'mon in. I have some leftover *pastisio*. My father's been on a Greek food tear since I told him you liked the food. I think he's going to try to win you over."

Zoe let them into the tiny bungalow. Extracting a foil pan from the fridge, she popped it in the oven, then set the timer. Leaving Max standing by the door fiddling with his watch, she went to the bedroom and eased off her Doc Martens and socks, stretching out her toes for the first time that day. Without warning, she decided a shower was in order, and darted in for a quick rinse with her favorite melon scented scrub.

The oven beeped after she'd slipped on loose fitting shorts and a soft cotton T-shirt.

"Why are you standing by the door? Sit, have a little food," she said, easing the pan from the oven.

Zoe got two of the mismatched plates that came with the rental down from the cabinet and added assorted silverware.

Max sat, but still looked wary.

"What?"

"But we're not a couple, are we?"

Zoe paused between filling the water glasses with iced tea. "Let's not do this. I'm here now. With you. We're both going through a hard time. Can't we comfort each other? You've made me feel a lot better. You've made me feel really good. I—" At a loss for words, she got back to pouring water and doling out the Greek version of lasagna.

Max ate mechanically, no doubt distracted by the hard choices he was going to have to face. "The nurse seemed like she had things under control. She promised to see that he got on the van for the adult day care. We visited three places today. You'll see more tomorrow, then you'll make a decision. No choice is final. If one place isn't to his liking or yours, then you try another."

Her dad was as great a cook as he'd always been, but like Max she'd lost her appetite. Clearing the dishes, she ordered Max to relax on her bed. After she cleaned up the kitchen, she joined him. Other than his shoes, he was wearing all he'd had on since the morning. Against his token protest, she undid his belt buckle, shucked his pants, and socks. Next, she eased the shirt over his head.

"Lay on your stomach," she commanded.

All out of fight, Max turned. His rainbow striped boxers made her smile. It was probably the first thing that had brought a smile to her lips that day.

Next to the bed, she had a small bottle of chamomile scented almond oil. Dabbing a little in her palm, she rubbed her hands together, then massaged his calves, then bent his legs at the knees, gently stretching his thighs. Hooking her thumbs in the waistband of his underwear, she removed it without a word of protest from him. The massage was doing what she intended, making him let go of it all.

The back of his legs, and tight little butt came next. When she went back to flexing his feet, her thumb grazed a little tattoo she'd never noticed before. Pausing, she strained to look a little more closely. A broken pocket watch graced his calf. *'Szerelem öl lassan'* was intertwined with loose cogs and a dangling chain.

A groan of relief or approval escaped his throat. Zoe took it as a green light and smoothed more oil, this time on the broad expanse of his back. She paid special attention to those little kinks and knots of tension between his neck and shoulders. His arms, the backs of his hand and talented fingers were next. "Turn over," she whispered.

He moved slowly; from lethargy or reluctance, she couldn't tell. Max might have been tired; his cock was anything but. Ignoring the one thing she wanted to massage most, she rubbed his chest, working her mind around the translation of the Hungarian words. Sometimes a little bit of language was worse than none at all. The only word she recognized was a form of slow because she'd asked people to slow down, when they came at her with rapid fire Hungarian, more than once.

Pouring more oil on her hands, she massaged his biceps, forearms, and palms.

"Hey, that tickles," Max said, his voice low and husky.

"Sorry. Are you ticklish?" she asked, marveling at what she didn't know about him. First the tattoo, and now this. But a few weeks of fucking was not the same as familiarity.

A single shoulder went up and down. "A little, maybe, but don't stop what you're doing."

Relieved to finally have his explicit permission, she scooted off the bed and knelt at the foot. She pressed her thumbs hard into his heels then pushed against his arches, trying to ease the tension there. Flexing his feet, she was gratified to hear cracking and another groan of relief from him. His thighs were next. Zoe worked hard to ignore the cock pulsing between his thighs, begging for her mouth. The small bead of fluid that escaped from the tip was too enticing, though, and she swiped at it with her thumb, then sucked the musky taste away.

"You're killing me, Zoe. That's the hottest thing I've seen since ten minutes ago when you put on that nearly see through shirt."

"Hmph," she responded, amazed he could string together that many words because her power of speech had been arrested. It was taking everything in her not to mount him like a desperate animal. Picking up the bottle and adding a single drop of oil, she rubbed her palms together, heating them up. She wrapped one hand around the base of his shaft, the other around the top. Then she moved them up and down in unison, pumping him. He'd been as hard as steel when she'd grabbed him, but he seemed to get even harder by the minute.

"You're killing me again, Zoe. Come here. Let me kiss you. Let me make love to you. I won't last long if you keep that up."

For a long moment, she warred with herself. She wanted so much to bring him pleasure. Max seemed like the kind of guy who'd denied himself pleasure for much too long. On the other hand she craved the oblivion that riding him would bring.

Max made the decision for her when he lifted the shirt above her breasts and each of his thumbs zeroed in on a nipple.

"Damn, that's so good." It was so, so good. She could get used to this.

"Don't I know it," he said. Bracketing his hand around the base of her skull, he pulled her down for a kiss. It was a sloppy, wet kiss that started out of control, and had them both panting in what seemed like seconds.

Both of them reached for the waistband of the shorts

at the same time. When she was as naked as he, Zoe impaled herself on the hard throbbing cock that had been tempting her. She rode him like a stallion as she braced her hands on the landscape of his broad shoulders. Max's fingers alternated between her breasts.

"I'm really close, Zoe," he breathed.

Her head fell against his neck when his hands left her nipples. One palmed her butt, moving her just that much faster, making it just that much rougher. The other found her clit. That tiny bit of friction sent her flying, stars burst behind her eyelids.

A minute later, the warm gush of his seed and the hoarse shout wrenched from his throat let her know he'd joined her on the other side of bliss.

She eased off Max and flopped on the bed, throwing her hand over her eyes.

"Zoe, I forgot…the condom. Are you—?"

"I have an IUD. No worries about a little Max or Zoe in nine months. I live life on the edge, but not that close to the cliff."

Max's "thank God," caused the tiniest twinge in her belly. Zoe needed to get the hell out of Southern California. Nick, Holly, and her dad must be rubbing off on her.

"Caring for my dad is enough right now. I can't imagine adding kids to the mix. There's not enough family leave in the world."

"Got it, Max. I hear you loud and clear," Zoe said, cutting him off.

Whatever else Max was going to say was stifled by a yawn as big as the chasm of the Grand Canyon. A few seconds later, he tucked a pillow under his head and was halfway to sleep.

Before he drifted off, Zoe poked him lightly in the shoulder. "I can't work it out—that tattoo on your leg. What are you doing slowly? Watch repair?"

"Do you know *ölni*?" he asked, his voice a whisper.

"A verb—to what?"

"To kill. It says: love kills slowly."

NINETEEN

Max

"What are you working on?" Max asked.

The drafting chair nearly fell as Zoe jumped a mile high. "You scared the shit out of me. What are you doing skulking around at four in the morning?"

"I wasn't skulking. I had to go to the bathroom. When I came back, I realized you weren't in bed."

"I'm used to living alone," Zoe said in explanation, shaking her head. "I've learned never to ignore the muse. She likes to play hide and go seek sometimes. When she asks to come out to play, I always say yes."

Halfway between wakefulness and sleep, Max smoothed a hand through her hair and down her back. She was back in the sexy little outfit she'd put on after her shower, but before she'd blown his mind with that massage. Thinking about that massage was certainly waking up certain parts of his body.

"You want to come back to bed?" he asked, all awake now and ready for a second go round.

"Maybe in a little bit," Zoe said, turning back to the white paper and black ink in front of her. She had a pencil behind one ear. Ink stained most of her fingers. He wondered if she ever got any on the paper. She was scratching the pen across the textured sheet, when he looked close at the drawing. It wasn't Budapest or Prague or Krakow on the page, but a single level house that looked very much like post World War II suburban Los Angeles.

His eyes snapped to the upper right hand corner. The place where the name of the strip was always placed. But her stylized lettering of Wanderlust was absent. In its place was Canoga Park. It was in pencil, yet to be inked. Max's eyes wandered across the table. There were three or four Wanderlust strips scattered about that looked halfway completed, pictures drawn, but the words were still in pencil. These Canoga Park strips were nearly done, though.

CANOGA PARK

By Zöe Andreis

CANOGA PARK

By Zöe Andreis

CANOGA PARK

By Zöe Andreis

By Zöe Andreis

"Is that the Valley?" he asked.

Zoe jumped again. "You've gotta stop doing that. I thought you'd gone back to bed." Forcefully, she snapped off the klieg bright light that had illuminated the desk. "I'll come with you this time, make sure you make it."

Max got into the blanket and duvet laden bed first, then lifted up the covers in blatant invitation. Zoe slipped in, curling toward him. She was quiet so long Max thought she'd fallen asleep. But she shifted her legs, and let out a long sigh.

"What's that other strip you're working on?"

"Nothing. Just a throw-away idea."

"What do you mean, throw-away? Looks like you've done some work on it."

"Not throw-away, exactly. Just something that probably won't go anywhere. I don't have a Beetle Bailey or Peanuts. Most strips don't have that kind of longevity. I certainly don't think anyone will be hard pressed to continue on Wanderlust after I'm dead. So I have to have some back up plans. It's not like I'm Mort Walker and have a big family to keep me alive after death."

"Do you want a family?" Max asked because he very much wanted one when the timing was better.

"I already have a big one. You've met every last one of them, I think."

"I'm asking if you want to get married and have kids." He was more blatant this time.

"I like to practice," Zoe said, derailing any further a conversation he really wanted to pursue.

Max was horrified when he woke up six hours later. Ten o'clock! He couldn't remember the last time he'd slept past six on a weekday.

This time, Zoe was fully dressed when he came out of the bedroom. Her drafting table was clean. Neat stacks of comics sat on the corner of the table. She was in the kitchen nursing a cup of coffee, and flicking through web pages on an ultrathin laptop.

"You're up. Coffee's on the counter. It's one of those cup things. Pick your cup. You have today off, right?"

"Yeah, more emergency family leave."

"So while you were sleeping, I found two more nursing homes that have space and the facilities to take care of your dad. I say we go when you're ready."

"You don't have to do this. I thought you were behind on your strip."

"Catching up. I sent off a week's worth this morning. I'm four weeks out now. I prefer six, but four isn't too bad. I have you to thank. The sex is keeping my brain fertile."

Max could feel his face heating. He'd never been that comfortable talking about sex outside of the bedroom. Zoe, it seemed, had no such reservations inside *or* outside.

"I'm going to go shower."

An hour and a half later, Max pulled up to the second of two facilities.

"They look like poorly disguised hospitals," he said after he'd parked and turned off his car.

"This one is better than the last two."

Max pointed across a grassy ditch. "The hospital is next door."

"Best of both worlds?" She shrugged.

The hospital next door was where doctors weren't able to save his mom, but that was another disclosure for another day. They were seated in an innocuous beige office and eventually greeted by Norma Diaz, a woman whose badge read 'admissions,' but should have read 'sales.'

"Welcome to Sunrise Haven," she said, shaking both their hands. They were led into yet another beige office. This furniture was chintz instead of industrial gray, but the aesthetic was the same.

"You must be Max Kiss. I'm here to tell you what we can do to help your dad. And you must be Mrs. Kiss. Such a great name, by the way. I hope he kisses you often," she said with a laugh.

"I'm Zoe Andreis," she said, shaking the woman's hand. When the woman looked at her hand and Zoe's, Max squinted. Ah, the ink.

"Well, anyway, I'm glad that you and your wife could come today."

"We're not married," Zoe said so quickly that the woman hardly had a chance to close her mouth.

"She's a friend helping me in my search for a place for my father," Max said, smoothing over the awkwardness in the room.

"Right. Okay. You can never have too many friends. Why don't we start with a tour?" she said, picking up a couple of glossy envelopes and ushering them out the office door. "Okay. To the right here we have our reception desk. It's manned twenty four hours a day."

"When are visiting hours?" Zoe asked.

"We don't have visiting hours. This will be your father's home. You would be able to see him almost anytime like you do now. That isn't to say he won't be busy when you come, but you're more than welcome to participate in any of the activities we have here. We find that when family and friends like you and Miss Andreis come to visit, not only is the transition easier on the new resident, they don't feel so alone. Even if you can't visit often, we don't want you to worry about your dad. He'll have the opportunity to meet other residents and share breakfast, lunch or dinner." She led them into a well-appointed dining room. There was no hint of the high school cafeteria or prison dining hall here. "Or if your dad's more of a solitary type, we'll be happy to bring him dinner in his room."

"Did Zoe mention on the phone that my dad is in the early...to middle stages of Alzheimer's?"

"Of course."

"Do you think he'll be dining or dancing or whatever with the other residents?"

"Alzheimer's and dementia don't mean they're bedridden, Mr. Kiss. We want them to live with dignity. So while some of their memories are slipping away, we hope they can create new ones while they're here. Speaking of which, let me take you to some of the special areas we've designated for residents like your father."

Max followed the cheerful woman through a series of corridors. The rooms were all brightly lit and tasteful. It was one hundred and eighty degrees from the first place he'd visited with its residents laying in cots in the hallways. That home had smelled heavily of disinfectant and things he didn't at all want to think about.

"This is our memory care center," she said. "Your father will be one of the residents who's been challenged by memory loss. We have a series of areas and services dedicated to residents with these kinds of special needs. First," she started, opening a door, "we have areas decorated in warm soothing tones. When one of our residents is having trouble during the day to day activities, we like to bring them here and focus on something positive. Whether it's one of our counselors talking to them about their past, letting them tell the stories of their youth, or even something tangible like arts and crafts. When some of our residents get…agitated, we try to engage in valida-tion therapy."

"What's that?"

"Here," the woman said, leading them to a small room equipped with a few chairs and a flat screen. "Let me show you." She pushed a few buttons and in seconds, they were watching a slickly produced video of an employee talking about how she steered residents away from discus-sions about loved ones who've passed into more concrete areas about their memories or experiences with that loved one.

"And if it's needed, we can have someone who can help guide your father through his daily routine. We also make an effort to get them into as many brain stimulating activi-ties as possible. Is your father bound by any physical limi-tations?"

"Except for his mind, he's fit as a fiddle," Max said.

"Well then, we'll be happy to enroll him in stretching, walking, or even yoga."

"It sounds like a cruise ship," Max said on their way out the door, laden with glossy folders and slick full-color brochures. The cost of that stuff alone had to be half of the steep price of living there.

"I know she was a little much on the hard sell, but that seemed like the best place we've seen so far," Zoe said.

Max nodded. "It was nice enough. I wonder how he'll make the transition. He and my mom were in that house together for thirty years."

"I'm not prying, but how can you pay for all this when a nurse was outside of your budget?"

"The house. For once I'm thanking God for the

stratospheric home appreciation in California. If I sell the house, the proceeds will outlast my father." It made Max immeasurably sad that this was the kind of calculus he was doing these days.

"How long did his doctors give him?"

"Five years on the high side," he said out loud for the first time ever.

"Oh," Zoe responded. He could empathize. It was what he'd thought the first time his father's gerontologist had laid bare the survival numbers. People always said they wanted to know when they were going to die. And by that they usually meant, they wanted to hear that they'd die in their sleep at ninety-nine after having completed every last item on their bucket list.

But that wasn't how it worked. Someone had to die in a war zone. Someone had to die in a car accident. Someone had to die of a random act of violence. Someone even had to die of a heart attack on a city bus. Death wasn't dignified. It wasn't easy. And most of the time it wasn't predictable, except when it was.

Into the quiet that had settled into the car, he said, "I was a late-in-life child for them. Men live a shorter time. Plus I think my mom may have done a lot to hide his symptoms, or at least she compensated for them. Or maybe his body stopped trying after she died."

Zoe squeezed his hand. "I'm really sorry about this."

"I'm just glad I don't have to go through it alone."

"Back at you."

TWENTY

Zoe

"Got a clean bill of health," Dominic said, practically crowing with delight. Papa did a little skip-dance in his tights around the apartment. She had to close her eyes and look away for a long second. For a moment, she had a distinct memory of her parents dancing in the kitchen. She'd come down in the night for a third glass of water, and they hadn't heard her. They danced flawlessly to a tune only the two of them could hear. When they'd started kissing, she'd decided she probably didn't need that water after all.

"She didn't exactly say you were one hundred percent, Papa. She said if you continue to follow the prescribed treatment and take the medication and don't do anything dumb, then you'll probably be fine."

"That, dear heart, is the very definition of a clean bill of health. I'm fifty-six, not fifteen. I'll take what I can get."

"What are you trying to say?" Zoe asked. Her father wasn't always the most direct person—at least with her.

Papa and her brothers communicated in some completely different language. Their dynamic was full of unspoken nuance that all these years later, she was *still* trying to figure out.

"I'm saying that you don't need to babysit me anymore. I'm saying that you can dismantle the chart you have stuck to my living room wall. I'm saying that I'll spackle the holes left from your drilling efforts. I'm saying that it's okay for you to go home."

"You want me to go? Already?" she asked. For some reason she couldn't put her finger on, his dismissal made her incredibly sad. Her father didn't need her anymore. She'd maybe liked being needed.

"I remember when you were about four years old, one of your cousins was moving out—"

"Who?" Zoe asked, ready to take a ride down memory lane, especially if it involved her mom.

"Your aunt Allegria's oldest girl. Anyway, you kept asking me why she moved out. Where was she going to live? It was like you thought moving out of your parents' house meant you dropped into a hole in the earth. On the way home, you promised me you'd never leave home. Your little face was so solemn when you promised to live with me forever."

"But I didn't stay," she said, trying to grasp at the memory. She couldn't quite picture the car or the details of the move. But she could remember how scared it made her to think of losing her parents, of being out in the world without them.

"No parent expects their child to stay," Dominic said. He looked away and chuckled to himself. "God knows when they are teenagers, you sometimes look forward to that day when there's no more pouting, sulking and back talking."

"Yeah, well. It was hard being the tall girl. But I recovered," she said. Not fitting in had made her moody for much of her teen years. That and the constant construction, but she wasn't going to rub salt into that sore spot of their relationship.

Her dad sighed. She hated that sigh. It was full of 'should have beens' and expectation. He said, "I love you and want you to be happy."

"I am happy, Papa," she replied before he could go on further. Why was it no one thought she could be happy without a husband, without kids, without the U.S? "I don't need—"

"Let me finish. I'm not going to pester you about a guy in your life or the fulfillment that kids bring."

"Thank goodness." Her head dropped in relief.

"I'll leave that to your Max Kiss."

"He's just a friend, Papa. He—"

Dominic waived her protest away. "I'd love it if you could be happy in Los Angeles," her father started. She tried not to roll her eyes. Next he'd go on about baby Iris, looking at her flat belly with expectation. He continued, "Look, we're from Chicago, a whole different kettle of fish from this place. The so-called City of Angels isn't for everyone. If you're happy in Budapest of Milan or Athens, then I'm happy for you."

"It's not like it's eighteen thirty-two and I got on a boat to the new world and will never see you again. I text you. You could text back, you know."

"I still can't figure how you can have a conversation like that. I never know when it's over. I always mess up the words. The automatic correction—"

"Maybe we could Skype?" The look on her father's face said the computer in his makeshift office wouldn't double as a videophone. She sighed in resignation. "I'll call you on Tuesday nights like I used to."

"I know," he said, pulling her close. "I know you will." Zoe pretended she didn't see him wipe an errant tear from the corner of his eye. "Now, let's get this board down and into the garage," he started, his tone full of brisk efficiency. "Maybe I'll hang it there and use it for project planning. Adonis is always on me about making sure I can see the big picture and not overbook jobs."

Dominic may not have been a fan of the computer she and Nick had bought him for Christmas, but it did work. After they'd put away the dry erase board, her dad got a putty knife and some kind of white goop. She turned on the computer and called up her frequent flyer account. The travel gods must have loved her, because she was able to get a last minute flight out of Los Angeles to Zurich two days from now, on Wednesday. She'd worry about the connection to Budapest later. There were a couple of friends she'd love to have dinner with in Switzerland. Closing the computer, she went to talk to her father. She'd need to pack up, alert her landlord, and arrange for a ride to the airport.

And talk to Max.

♥

TWENTY FOUR HOURS LATER, Zoe found herself standing on Max's doorstep. He'd answered her text, saying he'd be home around three thirty. She looked at her phone. It was three twenty-five. She took a deep breath and pushed the buzzer.

Overwhelmed is what Zoe felt when the door opened. All six foot whatever of Max stood there. His hair was damp. The smell of some kind of soap or cologne assailed her nostrils. His golden eyes looked her up and down. Then a slow smile widened his mouth. All of a sudden, goodbye was the last thing she wanted to say.

"Hello Max."

"Come on in," he said, stepping back and sweeping his hand as a welcome.

She accepted his hospitality and walked into the living room. She was careful to deposit her backpack on a small side table, and not on the floor where it could be stepped on.

"How's your dad?" they both said at the same time. Their laughter filled the room, echoing off the walls.

"You first," she said, unable to resist the urge to reach out and run her hand down the front crisp Prussian blue T-shirt covering his chest.

"I settled on Sunrise Haven. I have tomorrow off. His essentials are packed—pictures of my mom, his clothes, the bed they shared for forty years."

"You'll move him in tomorrow? That quick?"

"Yeah. I don't want elder services butting their nose in. He wasn't too keen on the idea, but it's probably the best thing for him right now."

Zoe very much wanted to volunteer to help him with

that. But the time he'd be moving, and packing, and unpacking, she'd be thirty-eight thousand feet above the United States, Canada, Greenland, then finally the European continent.

Max's hand wiggled her sneaker-clad foot. "What about Dominic? He okay? You zoned out there for a moment."

"Clean bill of health. According to him."

"What does that mean? He okay?"

"Yeah. He's good. It was a scare. Nothing more. Hopefully he'll walk a little more. Sit in traffic a little less."

"That's great news."

"Elder watch is over," she said in a booming announcer's voice, mimicking the reporters who sounded the alarm when it rained more than a single millimeter in southern California.

He laughed again. She loved that laugh. She loved making him laugh, replacing the frown life's circumstances had etched into his face. "The news in Budapest isn't alarmist over precipitation?"

"Budapest? Try Chicago. That was real weather without the dramatics."

"Maybe a lot of frustrated actors in meteorology," he said. The smile from moments ago was replaced with a sober expression. "Now that your dad's better, how long do you think you'll be staying?"

"That's kind of why I'm here."

Max sat on the couch. Slowly he stretched out his legs. His hands landed on his knees. "Tell me when."

"Tomorrow."

"How did you get a flight so soon?" he asked, leaning forward.

"Sheer luck, I guess."

"That's it, then," Max said, his voice eerily quiet.

"It was really great meeting you. You were the best part of my time here. I can't thank you enough for helping me with my dad. I don't know if I could have done this alone."

Silence greeted Zoe when she ran out of things to say. Ran out of things she was willing to say out loud. Max grabbed for her hand and pulled her down to the couch, next to him. Letting go, he traced the arch of her eyebrow, the bridge of her nose. She couldn't stop her bottom lip from quivering when his thumb pressed gently into the center. He replaced the finger with his lips. Zoe tried to memorize the feeling. His lips brushing against hers, parting hers. In the long nights ahead she wanted to be able to remember the silky feel his tongue, the taste of cloves.

"I want to take it slow, Zoe," Max whispered when he pulled away.

"I can't, Max. I can't wait. I need you now," she said. Emphasizing her desperation, she lifted the warm shirt from his body. The belt buckle came next, then the zipper. In a flash, he was naked, and regretfully, she was not. Max leaned back on the couch, all hard, hot man. His cock stood proud and tall, twitching with the beat of his pulse. He grabbed it, unable to resist sliding the skin up and down once, then twice.

It was the hottest thing Zoe could ever remember seeing. Standing, she decided a little striptease was in order. She wanted him to have something to remember, should he be lonely. Shimmying from her leggings, she took in the golden body, hard muscles, harder penis. No, he wouldn't be alone for long.

Pushing away that thought, Zoe turned, did a little bend and shook her unhooked bra to the floor. When she turned back, she was gratified to see him jerk himself one or two more times. Her nipples hardened in the cool room, the nighttime desert air brushing across her nearly nude body.

"The panties," Max croaked.

"My pleasure," she returned, doing another shimmy before tossing the black lace toward the nearest lamp. Her aim was accurate, and the room, which had been brightly lit, was cast half in shadow. Instead of hiding his body, the muted light emphasized the ridges and grooves of muscle and bone.

To music only she could hear, Zoe danced. She imagined she was in a dark club in Lisbon, *fado* music filling the room, a mysterious man who looked a lot like Max watching her.

"Come here. I can't take much more of this."

"I wish we had real music," Zoe said, taking tiny steps toward him. "We never did it to music." Laying a hand on either shoulder, she sat on his outstretched thighs and braced her knees on the cushions. Circling his neck loosely with his arms, she whispered in his ear, "I don't even know what kind of music you like."

Seemingly effortlessly, he lifted her hips. She took hold of his hard, throbbing cock, notched it, and sank deep onto him. God damn she was going to miss this.

Maybe she should have tried to stay another week. Or two.

They were still, joined, for a long moment. She loosened her arms and pulled back. She looked in his eyes. "I'm going to miss you," slipped from her lips. That wasn't at all what she'd meant to say.

His eyes closed as he tightened his grip on her waist. She shut her own eyes and tried to extract every last feeling and emotion from the friction between her legs, the smell of musk and sex. When a hand landed on her breast, squeezing and abrading her nipple, all thought about first times and last times and all times in between slipped from her mind. All left was here and now. His other hand left her breast and slipped between her slick folds, thumbing her clit. She nearly rocketed off him.

"Don't stop, Max," she cried out.

He didn't. Not for a moment. Not when she came the first time. Not when she hit a second crest coming again, this time milking an orgasm from him.

He didn't stop hours later when the lit candle next to his bed dripped massage oil into his hands and he did his best to reciprocate the massage she'd given him. Max didn't stop kissing, touching, loving her until the wee hours of the morning.

He was dead to the world when her phone buzzed at eight o'clock. She sat up and watched his chest move with deep even breaths. Long dark eyelashes lay against his cheek. She wanted to wake him up. But there wasn't time. She needed to meet her landlord, turn over the key. Nick was going to pick up her desk and put it in storage. If she ever came back...no, *when* she came back, she'd have a place to set up for work. Then she had to be at the airport by five thirty for the once per day flight. No, there was no time to wake him up. No time for awkward goodbyes.

She tiptoed to the living room, retrieving the clothes she'd tossed everywhere the night before. Then she plucked the backpack from the table where she'd left it. Lifting the lid of the wooden box she'd found at a shop on La Brea, she checked to make sure the 1950's Omega Speedmaster was as intact as it had been when she'd bought it from the market vendor.

It didn't look like much to her. Three large hands, three tiny ones. Zoe took a pen and notebook from her bag. Pen poised over paper, she scribbled 'Max.' After that she couldn't think of anything to write or sketch. She crumpled the paper and pitched it in the basket near the door. In socks this time, she padded to the bedroom. It took everything to hold back from sifting through his hair, or smoothing her fingers along his brow.

She pushed a deep indent into the pillow and nestled the box into it. Ticking off the long list of tasks in front of her, she found her shoes and pulled the door closed behind her carefully, not to make a sound.

TWENTY-ONE

Max

He didn't want to open his eyes. He didn't want to see what he knew to be true. Unable to resist, Max opened them anyway.

Zoe wasn't there.

Zoe wouldn't ever be there again.

He swept his arms across the bed, ready to stretch, when he hit something. Abruptly he rose, moving the sheets. Cool air rushed across his body. The smell that was Zoe tickled his nose and tortured his heart. Refocusing, he looked all around the bed. There pressed hard into the pillow was a square box. He lifted the box and swept the sheets again, but there wasn't anything else. She hadn't left a note with her phone number, her Budapest address, or even a goodbye.

Max lifted the lid from the box. His heart skipped a beat or three. It was the Omega Speedmaster. It was the one watch he'd always wanted. The one object he'd sought to make his collection complete. Here it was in his hands.

He lifted the timepiece from the box. Flipped it over. Probably all original parts were here. His heart beat faster as he imagined opening the case, probing among the cogs and gears. He'd be working on something handmade long before he was born. The idea of it amazed him. But it was cold comfort. Because neither his father, nor mother, nor Zoe would be able to share in his triumph if he were able to get it up and running again.

He set the box into the drawer of his bedside table. It was time to make the drive up to his father's house. This was one moving day that he wasn't looking forward to. He was about to open the book to the last chapter of his father's life.

"I'm Barbara Cruse." Barbara was a short buxom woman with a gray and blue flowered scarf around her neck. Her sweater was as bright blue as the morning sky. After a moment, Max extended his own hand. She looked at his father behind him. "And you must be Miklós Kiss."

"*Csókolom*," his father said, taking her hand in a chivalrous shake.

"English, please *Édes Apa*," Max implored. "*Legyen szíves beszélyen angolul.*"

"Oh, that's okay. It's practically a United Nations in here. What did your father say?"

"It's just a phrase old...um...mature men use in Hungary. It means, I kiss your hand."

"Oh, how wonderful. That's a lovely thing for you to say, Mr. Kiss. You're quite the charmer. I bet you're going to be real popular here. The ladies love a gentleman."

Max tried not to think too hard about the little old ladies in the center. His father wasn't here to date.

"Where's his room?"

Barbara practically danced over to the desk to retrieve a clipboard. "Mr. Kiss, you're going to be in suite five-oh-nine."

"Is that on the fifth floor?"

"Building five, room nine. Let's go there now. I believe everything was moved in yesterday. We tried to arrange things in a way you'd like. Let's go see."

His father was unusually subdued once they arrived. He patted his easy chair, wandered over to the pictures of him and his wife on the dresser. He peeked into the bedroom then came back out. His face wore a perplexed look.

"Where is your mother, Jenci? She made the bed, but I don't see her clothes anywhere. She was never good at putting her things back in the wardrobe."

Euphoria turned to a ball of lead in his stomach when his father called him by his dead brother's name. It had all gone too smoothly. His dad had gotten in the car without protest. He'd even been nice to Barbara when she'd greeted them. Now the rubber was going to meet the road. Afterwards he'd wonder if Bubbly Barbara had pressed some kind of bat button because a young woman in pink and purple scrubs swept into the room. Gently, she grasped his father's arm and steered him toward the wing-back chair in the corner of the living area.

"Mr. Kiss, tell me about your wife," she said in the most soothing NPR voice he'd ever heard outside of the radio.

With a much stronger grip than he expected, Barbara steered him from the room.

"We encourage visits from family. You know our policy is that the senior living center is your father's home. But I think it's best that you leave now. Your father needs time to adjust and that means he needs to lock into this new normal."

"Can I come back tomorrow?"

"You can do whatever you like. Our advice? Give it a few days, maybe a week. We'll call you if anything happens."

"But—"

"Have you been juggling and arranging your life for a while?"

"Of course. Dealing with elder care workers, nurses, and family leave."

"Do you have a wife?"

"Um, no. But I don't see what that has to do—"

"So it's all fallen on your shoulders, right?"

Max shrugged.

"What I'm saying is that it's time to let us take care of your father. That's why you chose us. We'll make sure he eats, bathes, gets exercise, socializes, and takes his medicine on time. It's what we do. We do it well. Taking some time for yourself doesn't mean you love him any less. Okay?"

Max nodded. Intellectually, he understood everything she was saying. It was going to be hard, though. He'd battled survivor's guilt for much of his life. Taking care of his parents is what he did.

"I'll get going then."

"Have a wonderful night. You're easy on the eyes. I'm sure you have a phone full of women's numbers. Call one of them," Bubbly Barbara was back. The last she'd said with a wink and a shove out the front door of the nursing home. Once in the car he looked to make sure he had a number for his father. It was there nestled among the long list of contact numbers. Someone from every conceivable department had made the list.

In the refuge of his car, Max was completely at loose ends. He had to laugh at the idea of a long list of admirers. The number of women willing to date someone who drove a bus for a living was surprisingly short. The one woman he'd love to call, whom he'd love to spend a free night with was...on a jet plane. For the first time since he'd gotten a so-called smartphone, Max was grateful for the purchase. He typed in his search request. The response from the Internet was almost instantaneous. There was a single flight from Los Angeles to Zurich daily.

The old John Denver song started and played in his head over and over again on the long drive from Simi Valley to the Los Angeles International Airport.

TWENTY-TWO

Zoe

She should have known that Dominic had let her off a little too easily. When her father wanted something, he usually got his way by wearing everyone else down. It was harder for him to get to her when she was in Europe, but with her within striking distance, he'd done it again.

"Papa, I only needed one person to drive me to the airport. I'm going home, not on a sojourn to Tibet or something."

"Adonis, Nick, come here and say goodbye to your sister," Dominic called out, ignoring her.

She was wondering how in the hell he'd done it. Here they all were at five thirty in the afternoon in the soaring entrance to the Tom Bradley International Terminal. Even the baby was with them. She didn't know a thing about naptimes or feeding a toddler, but she had to assume airport visits wrought havoc on a schedule.

The hug from Nick was a really tight squeeze. She'd always loved her little brother, even if they'd never been as close as she and Adonis had once been. Swallowing past the lump in her throat she said, "Great little girl you have there. I'll send her something from Hungary."

"You do that. I'm sure she'd love to get something from her aunt."

"Aunt. Aunt. Aunt," Iris repeated.

She placed a little kiss on the kid's forehead. She was kind of cute when there was no diaper changing and food around.

"Kid, we'll talk next time you're here," Adonis said.

It was still hard being so close to someone she'd avoided for so long. But her heart didn't beat as fast. The urge to run away wasn't as strong as it had once been.

"Let's."

Unexpectedly, Adonis pulled her in for a hug. "Your guy is here."

"My guy," Zoe pulled back and looked directly at her brother. Her voice was whisper soft. "Max?"

"I'm pretty sure that's him."

"Did Papa…."

"Don't know. But he's here and it ain't to see this mug."

"Your guy is here," Dominic repeated, pointing directly at a man striding toward them. There was no mistaking the broad shoulders, slightly shaggy hair. Today's polo was goldenrod. The man knew about color.

"We're gonna go. We love you. Don't be a stranger," her father said, herding her family away. She looked at Max. He'd stopped to lean down and say something to her father. Running or staying. She wanted to do both. Her plan for a stealth escape from southern California had been totally and completely foiled.

"Hi," she said. It was the single word she could think to say.

"Thanks for the watch."

"Getting a broken watch would be so not done for anybody else. You're the one person who would totally appreciate that."

Max got infinitely closer. Zoe wondered if she was going to faint. Her head was spinning, her stomach churning. She clasped her hands behind her back so he couldn't see them shaking.

What in the hell was going on? She couldn't remember anything like this happening in the last twenty years. That guy she'd had a crush on in middle school, maybe. Max didn't seem to be suffering any similar affliction.

"I'm going to miss you," he said, leaning down to kiss the top of her head. His hands smoothed her hair, caressed her cheek and shoulder.

Zoe turned her head away, to hide the tears gathering. Angrily she swiped at her eyes. "I don't do goodbye, Max."

"I kinda figured that after your disappearing act this morning."

"Why did you come?"

"Because I think I'm falling in love with you."

"We live on different continents. You know that. My job is living on a different continent."

"I'm not asking you to do anything. I wanted you to know how I feel. It's up to you what's next."

"I don't know when I'll be back."

Max braced her head, tilting it up an inch or two. She couldn't look away from his eyes, no matter how much she wanted to.

"I'm going to kiss you now. It's a really bad idea, but I can't help myself," he said. Then he did it. Tentative at first, he brushed her lips with his. Zoe nearly melted right there. All the want and need and desire was like a tangible thing between them. He deepened the kiss. It turned into unfinished business, and loose ends that needed tying up.

She was the first to pull away, not because she wanted to but because she had to. Saving her sanity was paramount. She pointed to the duffle still between her legs. "I have a flight to catch."

"I understand."

"I don't know what else to say, Max."

"You don't need to say anything." He backed up a foot. "*Jó utat kívánok.*" Bon voyage.

"Thanks. *Köszönöm szépen*, I mean," she finished with 'thank you very much' in Hungarian.

Zoe turned then and hefted her two bags, ready to make the long walk to the check-in counter, and the longer walk through security.

"Zoe!" Max called. She turned back for a brief moment. He was more than ten feet away now. "*Szeretlek. Szerelmes vagyok beléd.*"

His last words, 'I love you. I'm in love with you,' rang through her head for the next fifteen hours. She wasn't sure of the exact translation, but nothing he'd said had been missed because of her lack of ability in the noun verb conjugation department. When her head hit the stale smelling pillow in her apartment, his voice finally faded.

TWENTY-THREE

Dominic

"Well this is nice," Dominic said when he stepped into Bridget's house. What he didn't say is it was nice if you wanted the 1980s preserved in amber. He didn't need one of those TV shows that pretended to be the eighties. It was all right here like a mausoleum.

"You lack subtlety, Mr. Andreis. How about I show you the rest of That Eighties Show?"

"Thank goodness you have a sense of humor. I hate to tiptoe around," he said, relieved. You never knew with older people. Either they knew their shortcomings...or didn't.

"Maybe you can do a pirouette in those tights." Bridget lifted a single eyebrow.

"Ha, ha. Show me the layout," he said. Dominic was going to have to keep an eye on that one. She was as sharp as a tack.

It was a traditional three bedroom, two bathroom fifties ranch. It was the kind of house that used to dot Los

Angeles like the hay bales that littered rural Illinois after harvest. But the post war ranch was becoming as rare as a diamond. Builders were tearing them down and building mini mansions in their place at a breakneck speed.

"Great little place you have here," he said. "Have you thought about updating?"

Bridget's glance told him he'd put his foot in it.

"I don't mean there's anything wrong with it. I'm in the business. Everyone and their brother has remodeled their house at least once here. Knee jerk reaction. Sorry."

"Nothing to be sorry for. The house does need some work. Probably should dismantle the boys' rooms. One's back with his wife, the other has his own house. For a long time I thought there was a chance they'd come back. Cameron was back for a minute when he first separated from his wife."

"But they're back together?" he asked, trying to dodge a suspected land mine.

"Yeah. For good now."

"You don't exactly sound happy about that."

"She hurt him pretty bad a few years ago."

"Cameron, is it? The guy who put on the show when he picked you up that time?" Dominic asked. "Looks like he forgave her, though. The hurt doesn't only go one way, you know." Given that guy's brusque manner, he could see all kinds of miscommunication and bad feelings coming from a relationship with him. But he was wise enough to keep those thoughts to himself because mothers and sons and all that.

"Maybe you're right," was her grudging response

before she changed the subject. "I promised you dinner. You hungry?"

"I can't wait. How long until chow time?"

Bridget narrowed her eyes as if gauging his keenness for her cooking. "Ten, fifteen minutes."

"I'll be outside," he said.

The garage door had no lock. He lifted the heavy wood door, grateful it was a pivot design. Like a good homeowner, she had a ladder. It was wood and a bit warped on a couple of the cross bars, but it would do. He leaned it against the house and climbed to the top. A few of the shingles were missing. The flashing needed to be redone. He did some quick calculations in his head, then came in and washed his hands in the black and green tiled bathroom.

"What were you doing in the garage?" Bridget asked, hands in potholders on her hips.

"Taking a look around. What's for dinner? Smells good."

"Nothing as fancy as what you made. Roast chicken, potatoes, some green beans."

"My Midwest heart is glad," he said truthfully. It was the kind of meal that had been on lots of tables when he was back in Chicago. Los Angeles was a different animal. People spent nearly a quarter million dollars on a kitchen renovation without blinking. Then ordered take out.

She dished out a hearty portion for him, and a significantly smaller portion for herself. "I don't have wine. I hope water is fine."

"I'm easy," he said, winking.

"I sure hope so."

A little ripple went through his heart. He wondered if she was thinking the same thing he was. When she finally laid down the towel, her blue eyes didn't reveal a thing. Damn, he wasn't a teenager, but his mind still strayed to sex. Not as often as it used to, but enough to keep him interested.

"This is good," he said honestly. Her breast was surprisingly tender. God he felt like a randy effing teenager. Everything made him think of what it would be like to kiss her. He was too damned old for this. Forcing his mind to other topics, he asked, "What's the problem with the roof?"

"I'm not sure. It hasn't rained in forever. I think I saw some water coming in around the vent fan thingy in the bathroom. Maybe the corner of Cameron's bedroom too."

"That jibes with what I saw. Looks like you don't need a new roof, not this year at least. But I'm thinking the replacement of some missing shingles, and redoing the flashing in a couple of spots would fix you right up. Kick the new roof can down the road until an El Nino hits."

"How much do you think that would cost?"

"Materials only? Maybe five hundred? Maybe a lot less. Depends on whether I could find matching shingles."

"Oh, Dominic, I wasn't asking you to do it. Just trying to get a ballpark figure. That's much more reasonable. My neighbor across the street got a new roof and the blasted thing cost her seventy five hundred. She had to put it on a credit card."

"That's not a bad price for a whole roof, but for a few shingles, you don't need to be anywhere near that number."

"Such a relief," she said, rising. His empty plate disappeared into the sink. A slice of Boston cream pie replaced it. It was one of his favorites. He hadn't had the cafeteria standard in more years than he could remember. He was about to take Bridget on a walk down memory lane, when an unexpected kiss landed on his cheek, along with a dessert fork at his place setting.

"That was nice," he said baldly.

"Wasn't it, though?" Then an honest to goodness blush rose high on her cheeks. Well, now. Things were looking up. His favorite daughter may be on the other side of the world, but the future was starting to look a lot less bleak.

TWENTY-FOUR

Max

He'd made it through the first week. That walk through the airport terminal to the parking lot had been the loneliest of his life. Packing up his father's house in between shifts had mostly kept his mind straight. Zoe wasn't ever gone from his thoughts, but he had something else to focus on.

Today, though, there was nothing but missing Zoe. Over and over, he'd turned it in his mind. How could something so brief turn into something so important? He hadn't been looking for a woman, a relationship, or for love. He'd been working hard on making it through the days on the bus, and the nights with his father or home in Hollywood worrying about his father up in Santa Clarita.

The day of the week spelled out in the vintage Victorinox between the eleven and the one blazed Sunday.

Half the reason he'd thrown himself into his time with Zoe had been his desire to avoid his obligations. But some things fell to him and him alone.

Max knew what he had to do.

It was time.

Grabbing his keys and jacket from the table by the door, he got into the car. His audible, heavy sigh filled the cabin. It sounded pathetic to his own ears. Setting the car into drive, Max drove thirty miles north. He tried to let the monotonous scenery of alternating big box stores and chaparral lull him into a kind of meditation. A state of mind where he didn't have to tense up in anticipation of what he'd encounter. He tried to put himself into a frame of mind of acceptance for whatever was going to come his way this afternoon. It's what he'd counseled Zoe, but what he needed himself.

It nearly worked, keeping everything at bay until he exited the Ronald Reagan Freeway. But honking penetrated the cabin of the car. He must've unwittingly slowed down. Pressing the pedal to the metal, Max got to the… senior living center. Barbara and the others who'd done the intake had prompted him to use that name instead of old-age home, elderly warehouse, or nursing home.

The expansive parking lot and presence of nearby Mayo Newhall Memorial Hospital was a constant reminder of all that had led to this—his father being warehoused here like so many American seniors. Max stood in the lobby entrance for a long moment, taking in the familiar surroundings. The sight of chintz curtains and overstuffed couches couldn't overcome the smell of alcohol and disinfectant. With one deep breath after another, he tried to push away the dread that had settled deep into his belly somewhere on the San Diego freeway.

"Max! Great to see you. Miklós has been talking nonstop about family since you moved him in."

Barbara had introduced herself as an Associate Executive Director when he'd first met her. In his head, he thought of her as Bubbly instead of Barbara, because he'd never seen her without a smile on her face or a laugh bubbling out of her throat.

Bubbly picked up a clipboard from behind the wood structure that very closely resembled a hospital reception area. In his more charitable moods, he had to admit the place looked a lot like a mid-range hotel. Though, as he glanced around at the nearly empty lobby, he still thought the faux homey look didn't overcome the clinical nature of what they did here.

"Your dad's finishing up dinner at The Bistro. I'll have one of the attendants bring him to our reminiscence living room, unless you'd prefer the privacy of his suite.

"No, the common area is fine," Max said.

"Do you need me to walk you over?" Bubbly asked.

"I remember the way," he said, unmoving.

"Great weather we've been having this spring. The winds sweeping through the canyons have been delightful. The clouds have pushed clean air in from the ocean. I'm happy to revisit my favorite spring coats," Bubbly enthused.

He nodded in agreement, in farewell, and took himself over to the small side room dominated by a console TV, calico pillows, flowered upholstery, and boldly striped curtains.

"*Jó napot kívánok,*" his father boomed.

Max glanced toward the assistant who looked more

than ready to take his leave. "No English today?" he asked.

The man clothed in maroon scrubs shook his head. "Hasn't spoken English in a couple of days. It's the longest he's gone since I've been working on his floor. But I'm sure Barbara told you this sometimes happens."

Max nodded. Being warned that this may happen and having his father revert to his native tongue were two different things. "Thanks. I'll take it from here."

His dad had once been the tallest, strongest man in almost any room. The Miklós Kiss in front of him, shoulders hunched, leaning forward on the blue armchair, was no longer that man. The shift from father to patient hadn't taken as long as Max would have liked. It was as if his mother's death had flipped a switch in his father's brain.

"How are you doing, *édes apa*?"

"Kind of lonely," he answered in Hungarian. Max flipped a switch in his own mind from one language to the other. There was no reason to cling to English if this made his dad more comfortable. "I came here with your mother, but they won't tell me where she is."

Tension shot straight from Max's shoulders to the back of his head. He resisted kneading the incoming pain away. Despite his hope, this visit wasn't going to be much different from the others. "Mom died four years ago. She had a stroke and never came home from the hospital. Then you moved here," he said skipping over the bit in between.

Clarity returned to his father's hazel eyes. "Right. Yes, of course. Life here isn't so bad."

"Glad to hear it, Dad."

"But...the food isn't great. And," his father leaned even closer. He smelled of lemon soap and some kind of sweet dessert. Carrot cake maybe. "It's full of old people. They complain about aches and pains and their families not visiting."

Max laughed out loud. He had to nod in agreement with his father. It *was* full of old people. But his father was among the group, so he'd vowed to look at them as individuals. The way he'd want caretakers to treat his father.

"I'm here to see you today like I've come to see you before," Max explained in case his father hadn't remembered any of his visits in the last two and a half years in his house and now here in the same way his dad had forgotten his wife's death.

They talked for more than twenty minutes before Max's muscles relaxed enough to move his shoulders down from around his ears. Maybe it wasn't going to be anger and minefields today. His father was happy to chat about his days as a cobbler. His wonderment about people wearing disposable shoes. When had synthetic mesh sneakers replaced leather, his father queried. Then his father started in on flip-flops. It was another half hour before the shadows started to grow long in the room.

"I've fallen in love with a woman, *Apa*," he blurted out, surprising himself. These discussions were always one way. His father complaining. His father looking for his mother. His father broadcasting anger. It was the first time he'd volunteered something in years.

"Where does she live?" Miklós asked as if two-way conversations were the norm.

Max paused at the sequitur. He'd been counseled on

the sudden shifts a conversation with an Alzheimer's patient could take. But it still threw him sometimes when one coherent thought actually followed another.

"In Budapest, actually," he responded rather than try to bring up the weeks past. His father's short term memory was spotty at best.

His father's eyes lit up like candles on a Christmas tree. "A city girl, then?"

"I think she lives in *Erzsébetváros*."

"You don't know? Haven't you escorted her home?"

"Girls feel more comfortable meeting in a neutral place," was Max's non-answer. He regretted bringing Budapest's seventh district into the conversation. He'd been counseled more than once about focusing on the here and now to keep his father from falling deeper into the abyss of his disease. Explaining Zoe's disappearing act was the definition of unnecessary information overload.

"Is she pretty? Your mom was one of the prettiest girls at the *gimnazium*."

Max sat back and listened to the oft-told story of his mother and father's meeting in high school. How Zsofia Arany had pursued him. Despite adolescent hormones Miklós had dodged his mother's advances. He'd thought Zsofia wouldn't date him because the Kiss family was not-so-secretly agitating against the communist party while hers was full of highly placed ministers.

"Is your girl pretty?" Miklós asked again, more animated than he'd been in weeks.

"She's tall. Quite pretty. Very Greek looking."

"Turkish capture," his father murmured, shaking his head ruefully. "Longest hundred and fifty years in

Hungarian history." Max didn't remind him that the Hungarians had driven out the Ottomans in 1686. Going down that road could lead to a long Hungarian lament, starting with the Roman Empire, touching on the Treaty of Triannon and ending with the 1956 revolution. His dad may have forgotten most of his life in California. But Hungarian history imprinted on his parents and ancestors before, like ducklings on their mother.

"She's an artist," he offered, steering the conversation from the siege of Eger.

"Hungarians are some of the best artists in the world. The Flemish and Italians get all the credit." Miklós shook his head as if the Magyars had been all but erased from art history.

Max neither disabused his father of the notion that Zoe was Hungarian, nor did he indulge him in the artist debate. His parents had probably taken him to every well-known and lesser-known museum in the western world. The lecture on Hungarian artistic superiority could last for hours. Not as long as the lecture on the art of losing every war, but close.

"I think it's going to be time for an activity soon," Max said, watching the increasing commotion in this and the next room.

"Some kind of...smoothie...social," his dad said, stumbling over the now unfamiliar English word.

"That sounds like fun." Max tried to inject a little of the Bubbly's personality into his voice. No doubt she was jumping for joy in the lobby over the prospect of pureed fruit in a glass.

"You're as bad as your mother at pretending," his father scolded.

"Sorry. I have to go. I'd like to get some laundry done before I go to bed."

"So glad you came." Miklós took his son's hands in his. Age spots and wrinkles were the only visible difference between the fingers of father and son. "You've always been my favorite son, Jenci," Miklós said. Leaning closer, looking from right to left, his father's sweet breath tickled his face. "Your brother Max was always a bit too American for me."

Shoulders up, lump firmly in throat, Max placed a kiss on both his father's papery cheeks. "*Szeretlek*," he whispered. He did indeed love his father, even if he was the second favorite son—runner up to a dead guy.

TWENTY-FIVE

Zoe

"How was your trip to the states? We missed you last month. Did coffee and the English language theater. Didn't you say your family was from California?" Amelia Powell asked, not taking a pause between questions. They were two of a dozen women walking along *Bécsi út*, having toured Europe's first bed cinema. She could foresee a week of panels from that alone. Watching a movie in bed in your house was one thing, in a public building was another. An only in Budapest moment if there was one.

When they stopped at a busy corner, Zoe responded to the older woman. "From Chicago, actually. They relocated to L.A. after I was in college," Zoe explained. For some reason it bothered her for people to think she was from California.

"But you're back," Amelia said as though coming home hadn't been a foregone conclusion.

"I said I was coming back. I have three months left on my lease. Plus I have to plan a new adventure."

"Lots of expats go and never come back," she said matter-of-factly.

"True. Stacey moved there to be near her grandkids. Cristina too."

"What's your next adventure?" Amelia asked, hooking their elbows and leaning in conspiratorially.

"Krakow. I'm searching for an apartment now. Do you know anyone there?" Zoe asked. She liked to have a few contacts in new cities. Made the transition easier.

"My family's been all over the world following my husband David, but Poland hasn't made it on the list. You looking forward to it?" Zoe loved that about expats. They got it—her spirit of adventure. Amelia understood the excitement of conquering a new city.

"I'm going to bail on the next part of the tour. I've done it twice. Want to join me for coffee? There's a cute place—"

Amelia laughed out loud. "Europe is nothing but cute places. Let's peel off."

They left the American Women's Club members and stopped in front of Zazzi sat a few doors down. It was one of the new Parisian type shops that were starting to dot Budapest.

Huge glass windows, pretty display cases, and candy pink decorations made it stand out from the traditional intimate dark coffee shop that most continental Europeans seemed to love. They placed orders for coffee and pastries and chose a seat in a quiet corner.

Amelia's warm hand slid over hers. "It's been so great having you in Budapest. Young people keep our organization strong. We'll miss you."

The words tugged at Zoe's heart. God, was she getting maudlin and mushy in her thirties? Usually, she came, saw, conquered, and did it all over again.

"I met a guy while I was there," Zoe blurted out.

Amelia leaned back against the padded chair. "Considering the sheer number you've turned down here, this is curious."

Sipping her coffee covered up the stories she'd spun during her time in Budapest. Publicly she hadn't dated anyone. It didn't mean she hadn't been up for the more than occasional booty call.

"He was nice. I'd been hoping for casual."

"But it wasn't?"

Zoe made a project of sinking her fork into an Egyptian pyramid-like structure of dark chocolate cake and mousse. "I'm not sure."

Amelia tilted her head to the side. "Wow. You are the most confirmed bachelorette we've ever had in AWC. After that first meeting, no one's even dared to try to set you up."

"Want to know what's funny?"

"What?" Amelia asked, gamely abandoning Zoe's too loud declaration that she didn't do dating during her expat social.

"He's Hungarian. His parents left after fifty-six."

Her older friend didn't even crack a smile. Zoe wondered what it took to keep a straight face. She would have fallen on the floor laughing at the irony of it all.

"Name?"

"Max Kiss?"

"So very Hungarian."

"He told me he was in love with me at the airport... twenty feet from the check-in counter."

"Yet, you aren't smiling about it."

"I love how Canadian your 'about' is. Maybe I should do a year in the great white north. I hear Vancouver is nice."

"But not Los Angeles?"

"Who yells 'I'm in love with you' across a crowded airport? What in the hell was I supposed to do with that? We had a fling. I was leaving, and he drops that bomb-shell. It's been two weeks and I'm still royally pissed."

"Do you love him...back?"

"Who knows? I've only known him for about five minutes." Self-consciously she lowered her voice. English may not be the native tongue, but a lot of people under-stood it. "I needed an outlet. He was there. The sex was great. But that's all that happened."

"All? You responded to some e-mail I sent with a link to nursing homes you were visiting."

"Okay. I pushed him to pick a home. Social Services was on his doorstep. I don't think he realized how bad his father had gotten."

"Alzheimer's?"

"Yeah. You'd mentioned caring for your mom. Your advice was helpful. He found a great place for his dad."

"So you like him out of bed, but it's not love?"

"I have a career here—in Europe."

"You have a great job. There's no doubt about that. It's not like you're laying transatlantic cable or toiling in a factory, but is work more important than love?"

"I love my work. I have the ideal job. I get to write and

draw all day—in my pajamas if I want. I've worked for years for this. I'm at the top of the artist pyramid. Well, maybe not quite comic book artist or animator, but I'm damned close."

"And you can't do that from L.A. It looks beautiful on T.V. All blue skies and shiny cars."

"It rained once while I was there. Stormwatch was a crazy thing. All these reporters—"

"You're avoiding the subject," Amelia interjected. "I don't think you told me about your Max for no reason."

"What am I avoiding?" Zoe asked.

"Are you willing to make a sacrifice to try out a life with Max? I'm sure your dad wouldn't hold it against you if you moved out his way. Now that my kids are older, I miss them more than I love the adventure of travel." Amelia's revelation was a surprise. How many times had they talked about visiting out of the way places?

"But you're not in Saskatchewan."

"And neither are my kids. John's in Scotland. Julie's in Paris. David's got a few years left with Public Service of Canada. We'll probably go where the kids go."

"He's a bus driver, Amelia. I can't quite turn up on his doorstep hat in hand. He's got a dad to support, and I have my work here or in Poland, or wherever."

"Even I don't think that's a good idea. You both need to be strong, committed to a future. There's a compromise out there somewhere. He's not going to wait forever."

"I'm not sure he's going to wait at all."

TWENTY-SIX

Max

If there was one lesson Max had learned in the last few years, it was that life had a definite beginning, middle, and ending. The most unpredictable part was death. If someone had asked him four years ago what he thought the future held, he'd have said his mother and father would have lived happily together in old age and retirement. That they'd have died in their sleep at the same time.

It had taken him long enough to realize one thing, he would die alone—everyone did—but he no longer wanted to *be* alone.

Max parked his car on North Orange Drive, grateful that he had a keen memory of the Los Angeles landscape. In less than a minute, he was up the front walk and knocking on the door.

Zoe's father swung open the door before his fists could hit the wood a second time.

"Took you long enough." Dominic stepped back. That

was his cue. He followed Dominic into the house and closed the door.

"I had to settle my father in."

"Excuse me a sec," Dominic said, slipping his stocking feet into sturdy leather slippers. "I was about to have a snack. Want to join me?"

As casual as it sounded, Max understood the invitation wasn't the least bit optional. If he wanted access to Zoe, he was going to have to eat a little something. He followed Dominic into the kitchen and took the seat the man gestured to.

"Holly had this shipped from Eli's for me. Sweet girl."

"What is it?" Max asked looking at the wedge of dessert Dominic had deposited on his plate.

"A little indulgence. Eli's chocolate chip cheesecake. I used to sometimes take the kids there when it first opened."

Max accepted a dessert fork and took a few bites. "Pretty good."

"They say it's the sour cream. Do you love my daughter?"

The abrupt change of subject nearly sent Max's head spinning. He put the fork down and caught Dominic's eyes.

"I love Zoe," he said in as firm a voice as he could muster despite the nerves in his stomach. This whole conversation was a little old fashioned. But Dominic held the keys, so Max would play the game.

"What's your master plan? Because from over here, it doesn't look like you have one. You tell her you love her about five seconds before she gets on a ten-hour flight to cross the Atlantic Ocean."

"You heard that?" Max had intended it for Zoe's ears alone.

"Half of Tom Bradley terminal heard that. And no, I don't speak Hungarian. But there was no translation needed for that one."

Heat crept up Max's neck. Cool. He was cool, he told himself. He resisted the urge to tug at the collar of his polo. "I came here to ask for her number or a way to call her on Skype. She mentioned that she'd Skyped you when she was in Budapest."

"So, you call her, then what?"

"I haven't worked that part out yet."

"Here's what I see. I have something you want: Zoe's number, address, e-mail, online name. I give it to you. You call my daughter and nothing good comes from it. You say you love her, but don't have any plan. She can't just walk away from her job. And please don't take offense at anything I'm about to say. Know that I respect a man who works. But do you honestly expect my girl to give up her dream job? She can travel all over the world. She makes a fair amount of money and what, live in the bungalow with you while you're driving all around Los Angeles? No offense, but what is she supposed to do? Cook? Clean house? That works for my soon-to-be daughter in law, Holly, because she's that kind of girl. But I don't so much see Zoe dusting all day."

Max batted away the fantasy image of Zoe in the short-shorts she liked, feather duster in hand...cleaning his house and tuned back into the cold, hard reality of what her father was saying.

"I have a plan," Max said, forming the plan in his mind as he ate another two bites of cheesecake, working it out in his head. "I have a hobby that I've been thinking of turning into a small business."

"What's that?" Dominic said, looking him up and down, skepticism written all over his face.

"Luxury watches. I buy them busted, rehab them with original parts. Each watch would easily make me a profit."

Dominic scooted up in his kitchen chair. "I've never heard of this. Explain to me how this works. Sounds like flipping a house."

"It's exactly like flipping a house," Max said, then delved into numbers.

Forty-five minutes later, he had the information he'd come for. The great business advice had been an unexpected bonus.

❧

THE UNEARTHED AND charged up computer made that outer space noise that he didn't exactly associate with a videophone. Ten seconds ticked by, then twenty. He checked his watch. If it was noon in California, it would be nine o'clock in the evening in Budapest. He'd picked a Monday because it was the most likely day he'd figured that Zoe would be home. While he was thinking of how he'd find a better time to call, Zoe's face wavered then became fixed on his screen.

Her T-shirt was long sleeved, and her hair sat up in

short spikes, like she'd been running her fingers through it, but everything else about her was the same. Max's heart beat a little faster.

"Max? You were the last person I was expecting," Zoe said, settling into a ladder backed chair.

The classically Greek face, the husky voice that had shouted his name more than once in the heat of passion threw him for a loop. All he'd planned to say when he'd entered her number into the onscreen contact box flew out of his brain.

"Good to see you," he said in greeting, biding his time until his brain returned to normal function. Where Zoe was involved that could be anywhere from ten seconds to ten minutes.

"How'd you get my number? You never asked me for it. You said you loved me, then turned and walked away, Max," she said, calling him on his dick move. He'd forgotten that she didn't mince words.

"I saw your dad."

"Oh. God. How was he?" Reproach was gone. Concern replaced it.

"Dominic wanted me to tell you that he finished the bathroom. I saw it. The blue glass tiles are nice," he reported.

"Was it really done?" Her voice was more hopeful than a bathroom renovation warranted.

"One hundred percent from what I could see," he said, hoping that's what she was looking for.

"How did he look?"

"Hearty and healthy. He gave me some cheesecake — "

"From Eli's?"

"That was the name of the place."

Zoe looked off camera to the side, nodded her head. A second later, a glass of red wine appeared in front of her. Someone was there. Someone who'd poured her wine. Defeat lay heavily on his shoulders. He'd made no claim. Hadn't asked her to wait. Pressing forward anyway, he said, "There's something I want to show you."

"Over Skype?"

"Can you visit this website?" he asked, giving her the URL he'd bought. "There's a skeleton site there. I wanted you to see what I'm doing."

Zoe didn't disappear. Instead, she peered at the screen as if looking past him. She tapped and clicked a few times.

"This is cool. You should do something like this. Buy old watches, fix them, and sell them like new."

"Click the 'About' section."

He saw her look up and to the left. Her hands moved and clicked.

She read.

He waited.

In a minute, the biggest smile widened her mouth. She actually clapped her hands in glee. A warm feeling spread through his limbs as he basked in her approval.

"Oh my God. This is you. You're the watch connoisseur behind watchbuilders-dot-com?"

"The one and only," he said. Tuning out the sound of someone else rambling around her apartment, he outlined the business plan he'd put together. Sourcing watches, handling refurbishment, subbing out to his contacts from the swap meet if he went over his time. The more he talked, the more excited he got. When he'd taken the job with the MTA, he imagined he'd be there until the day his pension kicked in. He'd planned to start this business then —a fun retirement endeavor. Golf had never appealed to him, but this had. Meeting Zoe had ramped up his timetable.

"This is so cool. Is there anything I can do to help? Maybe some custom illustrations, gratis?"

"I'd love your help," he said smoothly. Step one accomplished. "But that's not why I called."

"Oh."

"I want you to come home, Zoe. To the U.S. To your family. To me." Max laid every last card on the table. What happened next was up to her.

TWENTY-SEVEN

Zoe

Eight Weeks Later

The email had arrived the day before. Her editor, Gwendolyn Hale, had loved the idea of Canoga Park. If she wanted to make the switch from Wanderlust to the new comic, Hale assured her she could sell it to as many or more papers than carried her current strip.

CANOGA PARK

By Zöe Andreis

CANOGA PARK

By Zöe Andreis

CANOGA PARK

By Zöe Andreis

CANOGA PARK

By Zöe Andreis

By Zöe Andreis

"Your strip was becoming a harder and harder sell," Hale had said.

"That's news to me."

"If you were going to keep on with it, there wasn't any reason to alert you. But given what's going on in the world, and the rise of the staycation, more readers have been tuned into what's going on in their own backyard, over what's going on in the world.

"Oh. So…"

"So, we'd love you to start with Canoga Park. We'd do a big marketing push this summer and debut it in the fall. That would give you time to move back to California and bank up a significant backlog of strips going forward. What do you say?"

Zoe said the only thing that came to her. "Yes."

By Zöe Andreis

Packing up was anticlimactic. She hadn't acquired much over the years. A good drafting table was sold quickly on the Used Stuff for Sale in Budapest website. In the end, it was her, two duffle bags, and one backpack at the airport. For some reason, she'd thought her near decade in Europe had amounted to more.

At the airport, as she stood in the long line to check her bags through to LAX, she started to worry. Staying with her dad would work for a week or two, but she'd need to find a place to live. Where she'd been in Europe, living had been cheap. Her American dollars had gone far for a comfortable home, eating out, travel, and other luxuries. Putting aside the high cost of an apartment, she didn't have a car, much less a license. Nerves that were normally absent beset her, making something as simple as lifting her bags on the airport scale a challenge.

She hadn't told Max she was coming back because

their last conversation had been like their first—no promises. Now that she wanted more than sex and distraction, could they start over again? More questions and worries plagued her in the security line. Again in the passport line. Why in the hell were there so many damned lines?

Rather than think too deeply about the yawning abyss of uncertainty that faced her, Zoe drank two large glasses of wine, chased it with a plastic snifter of port and slept across the ocean, and much of Canada. She woke during the normal turbulence over the Rocky Mountains. That signaled only two hours until landing. Using the mini refreshment pack, she brushed her teeth, wiped her face, and did the best she could to make it look like she hadn't folded herself into an airplane seat for the last however many hours.

The cab driver was happy to take her and all her bags to her brother's house. By the time the driver had hefted her bags to the front door, holding back her in-flight lunch was all Zoe could do. What had been a brilliant plan in central Europe had morphed quickly into the stupidest thing she'd ever done.

"Zoe? Is that you?" Holly called from the top of the stairs.

"I didn't call." She shrugged.

"Um, okay. Come on in. Iris is napping."

Like a trooper, Zoe hefted her bags up the long stairs to the living room. "I'm not planning to crash here."

"It would be okay if you were. The loft isn't made up. I can do it right now—"

"No, no. But I kind of need another favor." Zoe

ignored the fact that Holly was looking at her like she was a mad woman. "Can you drop me off on the corner of Sunset and Fountain?" She glanced at her functional man sized, not quite luxury watch, and peered intently at her brother's fiancé. "I kind of need to be there in less than ninety minutes."

Gamely, Holly woke a sleeping toddler, changed Iris' diaper, and bundled her into the car seat.

"So I'm going to drop you here, in the middle of Los Feliz?" Holly asked as she found the only available space in a loading zone.

"Yes, thanks. I'll come get my bags later, I promise."

For fifteen long minutes, she waited. An orange bus lumbered to the stop, the huge door folded in on itself. The driver looked at her, waiting. "You getting on?"

"No, wrong bus. Sorry."

In the twenty minutes before another bus rounded the corner, Zoe cursed herself a fool. This was by far the stupidest and most impulsive thing she'd ever done. She had no phone, not more than a few U.S. dollars in her wallet, and no Plan 'B.' When the second bus came, her heart beat a little faster. This had to be it.

It swung to the stop, and the doors folded open like an accordion.

Max.

"How much is the fare again?" she asked, boarding the bus.

"You owe MTA a dollar seventy-five."

Zoe pulled seven quarters from her pocket and dropped them into the fare box. Max steered the bus back into traffic. Zoe stood awkwardly for a few seconds then perched on the seat closest to the front door.

"Where are you headed today?" Max said conversationally.

"To the end of the line."

Her heart beat so fast, she worried she'd have a heart attack right here, doubling the number of passengers to die on Max's bus that year.

Max glanced at her occasionally, but didn't say a thing for five long minutes. She mimicked his silence. He pulled to a stop at the corner of Hollywood Boulevard and what looked like a park. Zoe watched as he tapped on the microphone.

"Ladies, gentlemen, we're going to have a five minute delay."

Amid the groans of a few passengers, Max turned off the bus engine, and unbuckled his seat belt.

Zoe's head whipped between Max and the bus full of passengers.

"What are you doing? You said you always kept to schedule."

He didn't answer. Instead, he grabbed her two hands in his and led her down the stairs and out of the bus.

"Is this a park?" They were right next to one of the huge dry desert looking parks that Los Angeles seemed to specialize in.

"It's the prettiest place I could think of along the route. There's something I want to say to you."

Zoe looked right and left. People were strolling. Dogs were walking their owners, and a bus full of riders were staring at them.

"Okay." She'd come this far. She was in it now. No turning back.

"Zoe Andreis," he started, then knelt on a single bare knee. "I can't believe you came six thousand miles for me, for us. I promise to always love and cherish you. Please say you'll move in with me."

It took her a moment to catalog what was happening. The pressure behind her eyes built, her nose itched, and her throat swelled.

"Say yes!" someone shouted from the bus through a crack in the window.

"This is so sweet," someone else said as yet another window was pushed open.

She looked from Max to the bus to Max again. What was she waiting for? He was offering her everything she'd hoped for.

"Yes. One hundred percent yes."

A collective whoop of excitement shook the bus.

Max glanced at his watch. "Oh my God, I've got to get these people on their way. I'm so late."

He'd never let go of her hand, though. With her hand in his, he rose and pulled her toward the bus. Once they were both on board and the door was closed tight, he pulled her toward him. She went willingly. He wrapped his strong arms around her waist lifting her an inch or two. Zoe twined her hands around his neck. Their lips met somewhere in the middle. She'd been kissed many other times and many other places, but this kiss on a bus in Hollywood was the sweetest ever.

Applause and the stamping of feet reminded her of

where she was. Reluctantly, Max broke the kiss, but he didn't break his stare for a long minute.

The rest of the ride was no more than a blur. On the side of a busy street, Max let out the final passengers, he unbuckled himself and pressed a few buttons. Then he leaned out the window to check the scrolling marquis.

"What does it say?"

"Out of service."

From there it was a fast twenty minutes to a bus yard in the middle of an industrial area in the Valley.

"Here are my keys. My car's in the lot," Max said tossing her a hefty key ring.

Another fifteen-minute wait had Zoe nearly bursting out of her skin with nerves. She laid a hand on one of her legs to stop the bouncing.

The driver's door opened. She handed him the keys. He started the car. They were silent as he left the MTA lot, driving a few blocks. On a deserted looking street, he pulled to the curb, turning off the car.

"I want to do this right. Without the audience," he whispered.

Max oh-so-gently laid a hand on either side of her face. She met him halfway for this kiss. Wrapping her arms around his neck, she tried to pour everything into that kiss, missing, wanting, needing, changing. They had to talk about what a future would look like. But for now, this was all they needed.

EPILOGUE

Max

Max couldn't help himself. He clapped his hands like little Iris did when she was excited about something. Suntanned arms dotted with ink slipped around his shoulders. He relaxed into the embrace. He couldn't imagine he'd ever tire of Zoe's touch, even if she'd managed to stain every single item of clothing he had.

"What's up?" Her voice was soft, husky. They'd worked in companionable silence most of the day. He loved that rusty voice of hers.

"I sold the Patek Philippe."

Her hands spun him around in the ergonomic office chair she'd bought for him and insisted he use. "Are you joking?"

"Nope. No joke."

"That hundred thousand dollar watch?"

"It was sheer luck picking that up at the estate sale. You're the one that spotted it," he pointed out. Zoe had dragged him to one Beverly Hills garage sale after another. In those first few months, she'd taken the business even more seriously than he had. After years of working for herself, Zoe was full of ideas and advice on going after what you wanted. He'd been tired, and a bit down at the slow growth of Watch Builders. They'd been halfway through this mausoleum some celebrity or another had owned since the time of silent film, when she'd pointed out the watch.

"All these people were oohing and aahing over some jewelry that they'd seen in an old film, when I saw the watch on a dressing table," she reminisced for about the hundredth time, but he didn't stop her. He liked hearing the story too. It was as incredible the hundredth time as it had been the first.

"I still can't believe that kid tossed it and the box in a plastic grocery bag," he said in wonderment.

"I got the feeling they didn't want to be there. I think they were great grandchildren of the original owner. Sounded like they all wanted to sell and get out."

"I'm glad that you carried cash on you." Zoe straddled him. The chair groaned. "I think we're taxing the weight limit," he said, suddenly not giving a hoot about the chair.

"What are you gonna do with that cash?"

"I've been thinking about that. What I'd do if that watch sold."

"And?"

"I think I want to take the business full time."

She smoothed a hand through his hair. "This is not me pushing you. Your job is important to you. I don't want you to quit on my account. I'd love you no matter what you did or do. Do you hear me?"

"You were right, though. It wasn't my dream. Until I met you, I didn't think someone could actually make a living at the thing they most enjoyed. It's like a dream come true."

"You're my dream come true," she said.

"Can I ask you a question?" Max asked. Her hips grinding against his was making him crazy. In another minute or two he wouldn't be capable of speech, but there was something he'd been dying to know.

"Anything."

"Is that couple in Canoga Park based on us?"

"They're married, with a precocious kid. They live in the suburbs and—"

"Answer the question, Zoe." He had to know if they wanted the same things. If they were finally on the same ink stained page.

She lowered her lashes. He tilted her head up.

"Yes," she whispered, then leaned in to kiss him. But Max had gotten hip to her evasion tactics. If she didn't want to talk about something or was feeling emotionally vulnerable, sex was her go-to distraction. Reluctantly, he leaned back the tiniest bit.

"I hope that's the answer to the next question I'm going to ask," he whispered.

He let her kiss him then. The question and answer could wait until a little bit later. For once, she wasn't going anywhere.

The End

Thank you for reading **Stirred**. I loved this one. Zoe is a cartoonist and I had the best fun working with an artist to develop her funniest strips.

You can see them here at zoeandreis.com.

ACKNOWLEDGMENTS

I don't usually write acknowledgments because, dear reader, I think it's common knowledge that no writer goes it alone (at least part of the time). As always, I'd like to thank my wonderful editors Laurie Larsen and Kay Springsteen. They've been my personal cheering section throughout many books.

I'd also like to thank those authors who support me everyday and keep writing from being a solitary endeavor, Maggie Marr, Beth Yarnall, and the Unicorns. We all talk online and in person nearly daily. I love that they don't think I'm crazy.

Last, but certainly not least, I have to thank Josh Bauman. Zoe's comics could not have come to life without him. He worked tirelessly and with great cheer throughout the summer (he in Berlin, I in Budapest) to bring Zoe Andreis' musings to light. He had great ideas and propped the comics up where I fell down.

I grew up in an era when a daily paper was a regular part of morning life. Whether that was the New York

Daily News, or the Hartford Courant, every morning there was a little peek at life and humor through what my late grandmothers called the funny pages. I hope that Josh and I honored the amazing talent and craft that goes into bringing a smile or a laugh to readers around the country and around the world.

To view more of Josh's amazing work, please visit him at www.joshbauman.com.

ABOUT THE AUTHOR

I write crazy, beautiful love stories because I believe story-telling is magic. I love complicated heroines with secrets, strong heroes who fall hard, and a long winding road to happily ever after. When I'm not writing, I love to travel to witness the diverse tapestry of humanity, photograph the beauty of the world, visit museums, and watch live theater. I live in West Hollywood, California ten miles from the nearest airport.

❦

I'm the host of Fifty First Dates the Podcast. I haven't found my own happily ever after, but I'm not done looking. Join me as I try to find my Mr. Right or maybe Mr.

Right Now in Southern California. #50firstdates #joliemoore #crazybeautifullove

www.ingramcontent.com/pod-product-compliance
Lightning Source LLC
Chambersburg PA
CBHW031554240626
47153CB00002B/500